D0065438

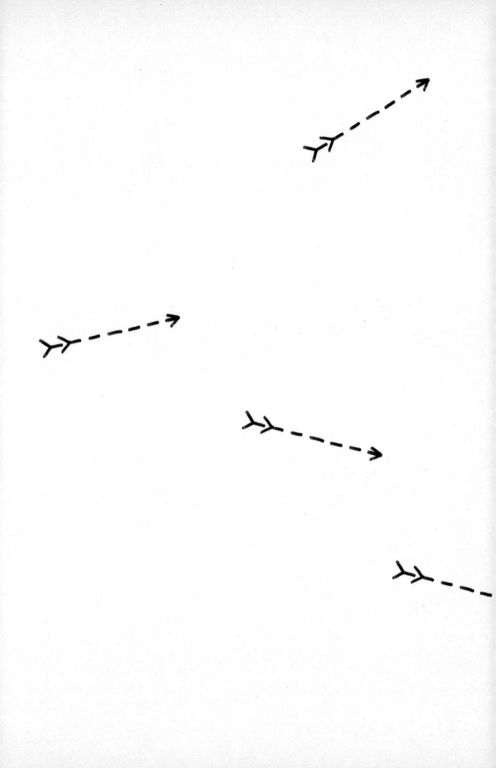

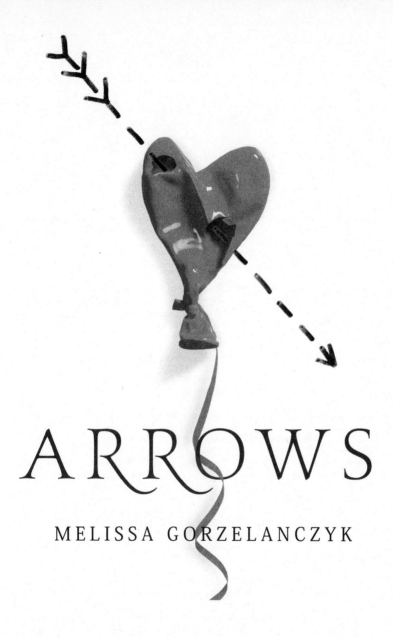

ARROWS

MELISSA GORZELANCZYK

DELACORTE PRESS

Text copyright © 2016 by Melissa Gorzelanczyk
Jacket photograph copyright © 2016 by Getty Images

randomhouseteens.com

Educators and librarians, for a variety of teaching tools, visit us at
RHTeachersLibrarians.com

Library of Congress Cataloging-in-Publication Data
Gorzelanczyk, Melissa.
Arrows / Melissa Gorzelanczyk. — First edition.
pages cm
Summary: Dance prodigy Karma Clark's unrequited love for Danny is unbearable until Aaryn, son of Cupid, tries to fix his mistake and ends up falling in love with the beautiful dancer from Wisconsin who can never love him in return.
ISBN 978-0-553-51044-7 (hc) — ISBN 978-0-553-51045-4 (glb) —
ISBN 978-0-553-51046-1 (ebook)
[1. Love—Fiction. 2. Dancers—Fiction 3. Gods, Greek—Fiction.] I. Title.
PZ7.1.G67Ar 2016
[Fic]—dc23
2015008992

The text of this book is set in 11.5-point Apolline.
Book design by Stephanie Moss

Printed in the United States of America
10 9 8 7 6 5 4 3 2
First Edition

FOR SHEA,
whose love empowered me

ARROWS

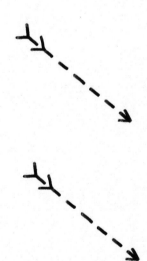

CHAPTER 1

AARYN

We landed at the edge of a high school parking lot, me with two arrows in my pack. Phoebe let go of my hand to scope out the area, appearing indestructible as she lifted her bow.

"Okay, Aaryn," she said. We'd just met five minutes earlier, though she was one of the cupids all the students had heard about. She gestured with her chin. "Them."

Arcs of golden light swam through the arrow she nocked into her bow, and when she retracted, the fletching made a dent against her cheek. Her kohl-lined eyes focused on a couple standing by the door of the high school, dressed up for their homecoming dance. They had no idea what was coming.

The girl, a short redhead in stilettos, darted quick glances at her date, who was wiping his palms on his suit pants. Freakishly tall, that guy.

Phoebe paused. With a snap, a glittery path tore through the air. The arrow disintegrated with a burst of light through the boy's tie. Phoebe half smiled as her arms relaxed.

"Well, Son of Eros—have you ever experienced the arrows like this?" she asked.

"No. Just target practice. Dead arrows."

She stood beside me, and for a second I felt awesome, getting one of the prettiest goddesses as my proctor.

"How cool is it that we ended up together on finals day?" She winked. "You're just the god I was hoping to get."

"Oh, uh, really?"

"Mm-hmm. Tonight is definitely helping my status."

"Glad to hear it." I cleared my throat, anxious to get on with the test. She seemed cool, though. Maybe she'd want to get to know me once I graduated.

With a satisfied smile, Phoebe placed a second arrow against the silver wire and brought the redhead into her sights. She did this little square-up-and-hesitate thing with her shoulders. The arrow flew and disappeared. Direct hit.

Things got pretty ridiculous from there. The teens held each other for a long time, the guy bending to her height, smoothing her hair out of the way so they could have an all-out tongue war. And then the reality of it all struck me.

Love was beginning to unfold out there, actual love. No one else in the world would matter as much to them as they did to each other. Two humans who hadn't even reached adulthood, who'd barely started to learn about life, and they'd already found their soul mates. In Lakefield, Wisconsin, of all places.

I scanned the parking lot, which was as dead as the nearby farm field. "Who am I supposed to shoot?"

"Well." Phoebe smiled. "I was thinking I should help you find the perfect couple. That's not my job, just so you know— but I'd love to do a little favor for you. Eros would appreciate that, I'm sure."

"I'm going to check out the school."

"You can't open the doors."

"No one's around," I said.

"Aaryn. Wait. You know the code."

I rocked on my heels, annoyed that she was right. The code about not opening doors was one of many the gods followed. *Never draw attention to yourself among humans.* A door opening by itself? Humans got creeped out by stuff like that.

Then another girl's voice. I swung my quiver around on the leather strap across my chest. Two more teens were there. The girl, a brunette, threw her arms around the redhead—shocker, she'd stopped kissing the tall guy—then leapt to catch up to *her* date, some idiot wearing a suit coat and baseball cap. A real romantic.

I slid an arrow from my pack. It glowed brightly, a steady, vibrant orange.

"Ready to join the ranks?" Phoebe asked. Pride filled her voice. The light from my arrow cast shadows beneath her eyes.

And my targets? Too easy under that powerful parking lot light. The girl was smiling, acting like her date was the most interesting person in the world, though she seemed like the interesting one: athletic body shown off by an airy pink dress.

I snorted under my breath as the guy's voice carried into the darkness. "You're so sexy, Karma," he said. Ha. What a name. Humans actually believed in stuff like karma. Mr. Romantic pulled her in, massaging her back as they kissed, his hands creeping lower and lower until they curved over her ass.

I sighed, then closed one eye. Everything around me blurred except the girl. This was it. My first match. The metal between my fingers glowing, the power to change someone's life forever. Yes, I was the son of Eros, privileged, but like everyone else at finals, this match was the beginning of my legacy. For a second my chest felt like it was going to explode.

I let go.

The arrow melted into the girl's back, a bull's-eye shot. The effect was immediate. She gasped when the kiss ended and her hands slid up his neck, slow and slinky. The power of the enchantment had struck. I drew out my last arrow, which had been matched as a pair. The arrows were made that way—made for each other, just like their targets.

"What the hell—" I held the arrow up. It wasn't glowing.

Phoebe started as I flicked my thumb on the blunt end. "Wait a minute, is that . . . ?" She snatched the arrow and shook it, like that might help. "A practice arrow? Is this some kind of joke?"

The guy began to lead his lovesick date into the back of a pickup truck.

"There's still time, right?" I said. "Let's just head back for a replacement arrow. There must be some record of the pair."

Our eyes met as we checked the Hive, our social web, accessible to us with a single thought. One thought—a power button—and we controlled a galaxy of information with our minds. The rectangular display inside my mind lit up, ready to search.

"No way." The arrow ration house had closed seven minutes ago.

Phoebe's hands covered her mouth.

"How could this happen? I can't let you go to Blackout, Aaryn, I can't. This is—"

"Don't get crazy. I'm not going to Blackout. Dad wouldn't let them do that."

"This is serious. You can't pass finals. You really can't pass.

Leaving a human like this, only one of them shot, it's like—the worst possible failure." She made a wild hand motion. "This is going to ruin me."

"Jeez, don't panic yet."

"I'm not panicking!"

Perfect. I twisted the end of my bow against the pavement, though I had to admit my pulse had sped up.

Blackout.

Where the failed gods go.

"How could you forget to grab a matching pair?" Her voice was getting shrill.

"Relax. This isn't my fault."

"You didn't let your pack out of your sight, right?"

My bow stopped spinning. I couldn't tell her I'd been distracted by the Hive or that I'd gone into a private comb to compare proctors with my buddy Chaz. She'd think I was a complete idiot. "I kept my pack right here the whole time," I lied, tugging the strap.

The girl was laughing again, her head popping up for a second as Mr. Romantic shook out a quilt and handed her the corner.

"What am I going to do?" Phoebe said. "If the assembly finds out . . . No, they can't, we have to lie. They can't find out."

They were sitting up now, facing each other, him leaning in to nuzzle her ear. Time on Earth seemed to slow. At least the guy appeared to like her.

"Do you, uh, know anyone? Who went to Blackout?" My voice was low.

"No. Of course not. Never."

Where the failed gods go as humans, their memories wiped.

The teens were kissing again, and then they flopped out of sight. *Thump.* One of them bumped the truck bed.

"This is what we're going to do." Phoebe squeezed my arm until it stung, but I didn't bother pulling away. "No one is going to find out about this. Got it? No one."

"Do you think she'll be okay?" I nodded at the truck.

"Oh, um, I don't know, maybe—whatever! Forget about them. I'm going to say you passed. You passed, okay? If the assembly finds out about that arrow, there will be no mercy. It won't matter whose son you are."

I swallowed, though it felt like a knife was picking at my throat. "You're the boss. Tonight never happened."

Phoebe slid her hair behind her ears and took a shaking breath. Her gauge earrings made her face seem fierce. "This is really bad, I'll admit it, really, really bad, but it's going to be okay, I promise."

"Well, hey—not everyone gets a happy ending." My parents, for instance.

"We have to get out of here." Phoebe grabbed my hand and yanked. Within seconds we had sliced through the atmosphere and returned to Mount Olympus, fog-breath circling our feet. There was white all around us, silver, gold, and stone. The land of the gods. We stood in the enormous corridor in silence, two cupids, though it didn't feel awesome the way I'd expected. Phoebe's emerald eyes were still watery, her hands trembling. She swallowed, which sounded more like a gulp.

"So, um, yeah . . . happy you passed?"

The question left a sour feeling in my stomach. That girl down there. Her life had changed, all right. My fist fell slack. "Yeah. Finals. Wow."

"You'll be a good cupid," she added, almost like an apology for how the night had gone. "Everything will be fine, see? No one even knows we're back. And you—are you okay?"

"I'll be fine."

"To think I almost lost you tonight. Oh my God, I shouldn't even be saying that up here."

Her anxiety was getting to me. A tight, suffocating feeling began to clench my chest. I stood tall, tried to get rid of it. I was a cupid, finally, after all those years of working my ass off. And hey—the three-year age gap between Phoebe and me had become irrelevant. Yeah, I was younger, but we were equals now. We'd botched finals together and survived. Maybe chocolate and flowers would help her feel better.

I offered her my arm, but the tight feeling stuck. "Let's see if there's a party."

CHAPTER 2

KARMA

One year later

I sped home from school with the window all the way down. The rain was more of a drizzle and helped kill that familiar, sleep-deprived floating feeling. A sense of calmness filled me.

Fall was coming.

The trees along the road were already fading from green to golden. Summer in Lakefield had lasted too long, and it had been such a hot, hard summer. Maybe I couldn't escape what had happened in the past year, but change was in the air and it felt amazing.

At home I was greeted by the sound of Nell screaming from my mother's arms. My sweet baby's fists pummeled the air to the beat of her cry until all the weight I'd shed on the ride home pressed down on my chest, reminding me. Fall couldn't change that.

"Sorry I'm late. Mrs. Smith let me stay after for extra credit."

"Did you know Danny bailed on babysitting again?" Leah said the second I walked in. She sat at the table, her arms crossed. "It's one night a week. One night, which isn't that hard, if you ask me. You should yell at him. If he was my boyfriend, I'd definitely yell at him."

"No wonder you're single."

"Whatever. He's a bad dad."

"At least he's in the same state as Nell."

"Girls," Mom said, her voice firm.

I shot my younger sister a look but kept my mouth shut for Mom's sake. She hated when we fought about Dad. And Danny? Leah didn't realize how busy he was. She placed our own father on a pedestal while beating Danny up over every little thing. I'm not sure if she just missed Dad, or was stupid, or what.

"Come here, baby." I shrugged out of my backpack and brought Nell to my shoulder, relaxing at how warm and snuggly she felt. At three months old, she was average for weight but already in the top percentile for height. Maybe a future dancer. Her gasps tickled my cheek.

"I'm going to feed her," I said.

"I just fed her fifteen minutes ago." Mom's lips pressed together. Was that the same flyaway ponytail she'd scraped up at five a.m.? Our days started early, thanks to my before-school dance class, but maybe she needed a break. She definitely needed a shower.

"Shhh, shhh, shhh. What's the matter, baby? Shhh, shhh, shhh." I flicked my gaze to the flowery clock above the fireplace. We lived in a decidedly female house full of pinks and purples and flowers and lace. That's what happens when your dad ditches you and moves across the country. You build up a fortress of girly things so no man ever hurts you again. (Mom's thinking, not mine.)

"I hate to ask, but can one of you watch her?" I did hate to ask. I hated it because they were going to think the worst of Danny, and then me, thinking I should probably just stay home with my baby for the night. Homework? That would have to wait. I promised myself I wouldn't fall asleep until it was done.

Mom was giving me the Look.

You're the one who got yourself pregnant and I've already raised two babies of my own and I'm not impressed with your choice in men, either.

That look.

"I have plans tonight," Mom said. "If Danny had given us more notice, maybe we could have worked something out."

"Can you rock her or something?" Leah called. "I can't even think." Her homework was spread across the table, where it had probably been since three o'clock. I couldn't remember the last time I'd had the luxury of an hour to casually tinker with my homework, messaging friends the whole time and telling other people what to do. I slammed my bedroom door.

Ugh! The ripping sound as I pulled Nell's fist out of my hair, and the sting of the whole day, amplified in that moment, made my vision blur and shift. I swallowed.

Lifted my chin.

I would not cry. Not now.

I sat on my unmade bed and called Danny. Talking to him always made me feel better on days like this. Days when everyday life, silly things, really, felt overwhelming. I listened to the familiar sound of his voice mail in one ear, Nell's cry in the other. He was probably busy with homework.

Or not, whispered a niggling voice in my head. I silenced it by looking at Nell, our baby. Our masterpiece. Her pink cheeks, her hair that curled at the ends, those adorable fat legs.

Danny and I were solid. We'd survived the one thing that killed most relationships at our age. Even being teen parents, our love was real. I'd known that since the first night we kissed.

The door popped open.

"Knock, please," I said, but my sister skidded inside, hands on her hips. She was all drama—thrift store designer clothes, dark hair styled like she'd had a professional team on the job, mouth set in a confident twist. In a family of brown-eyed girls, hers were the darkest. The thick eyeliner and sage shadow? More drama, which matched her current mood perfectly. My eyes were lucky to get a few swipes of mascara, since I didn't have time for makeup anymore.

"What did he say? Did you call him? You can't keep bringing Nell to dance."

Her tone was pointed, but there was a hint of pity in it, too.

"He's been really busy." I focused on Nell, because I couldn't stand my sister's judgmental gaze. Poor Nell. She'd been crying so often, especially at night. Rehearsals were tough. School was tough. Danny probably would have been better off dating a zombie. I really needed more sleep.

"Karma, you can't let him get away with this crap. He should help you more. It's like you're not even the same person you used to be. I can't believe he still treats you like this."

"Danny supports me. You know that." But my voice shook. Help me more? How about spend more time with Nell? He could if he really wanted. I patted Nell as guilt snuck in for thinking that. She continued to fuss.

"You need to make him man up. The way he ignores

you, then shows up like some kind of clueless hero? It's very annoying."

I gave a short laugh, but there was nothing funny about her statements. Leah was right, not that I'd ever tell her that. I stared at my bedroom wall as a feeling of loneliness crept over me. Loneliness and longing. Everything had changed so fast. One pregnancy test confirmed. One scholarship lost. Me, a ballerina, tripping through life.

I took a deep breath and gathered Nell against me, standing in ballet fifth position with my legs in a demi-plié, heels touching. Together we listened to the rain, a soft scratching sound.

"I'll talk to him," I lied. "Stop worrying. Stay out of my love life, and next time knock."

I glissaded across the part of the floor that was clear of laundry, exaggerating the movements with Nell in my arms.

"Your room is such a mess," Leah said before she left. She was right again. The clothes and papers and too many things I'd saved littered all the flat spaces. At least Nell's corner of the room was organized. I kicked at the stack of diapers that was tipping until they were straight. I'd get around to picking up the rest eventually.

Nell fell asleep. I continued to glide where I could, little leaps back and forth between the door and her crib, finishing with an improvised ballet bounce. Those blond lashes against chubby cheeks. Perfection. I tucked her inside the baby carrier with a kiss and dug around until I found my dance bag, her diaper bag, and my overstuffed purse.

Mom had relaxed in the recliner with a copy of *Better Homes and Gardens*. She looked up with tired eyes. I'd inherited her eyes, crescent-shaped. They always seemed kind, even when she was exhausted. She was the natural-beauty type, but her eyes were bloodshot now because of me—because of my baby—and because Mom was the kind of parent who would never leave her kids when they needed her and move across the country, even if what they needed was a lecture. Even at five in the morning.

"I'll be back around ten," I said.

Mom was trying not to look guilty over the whole baby-sitting problem but failing. She rubbed the knees of her yoga pants. "At least she fell asleep, right?"

"Mom, you don't have to watch her all the time. You're right."

"I want you to follow your dreams. I just—"

"Mom. It's okay. She's my responsibility."

"Next week, I'm calling Danny myself," Leah muttered.

Outside, the sky was incredible. Yes, I was weighed down like a packhorse, but wow. I stopped for a second to enjoy it. Rain glittered on the grass and trees like hope. I snapped the baby carrier into the base and headed to the studio.

"You brought Nell?" Peyton, my best friend, pounced on the carrier the moment I walked in, her mouth in an O shape. "Oh my gosh, she's so sweet I could die." She was always on the verge of dying around Nell. The studio was empty except for us.

"Danny canceled again."

Peyton ran her finger over Nell's cheek. "Did you guys fight about it?" She raised one eyebrow, which was auburn to match her hair. She was outdoorsy and always sunburned, since her complexion refused to tan. "He bailed last week, too."

"He could do a lot more for her," I said. A bad feeling was

stuck in my throat, like I couldn't stand what I was saying about him. "He's got his own future to worry about, I guess."

"If Nick left me to take care of our baby by myself all the time—if we ever have a baby, I mean—I'd be mad as heck." Peyton didn't swear. Instead, she pointed to add effect to her words, jabbing the air for *heck*. She sat cross-legged on the studio floor and cracked open a bag of potato chips. "I can talk to Danny if you want."

"That would not end well."

"Want one?" She held up the bag.

"No. I'm maintaining." I knelt beside her, shrugging the rest of my bags to the side. "How are your ankles feeling, by the way?"

"Eh, sore, as always."

"There's still time to heal before the scholarship competition. There are ten of them up for grabs, you know. Not just the big one."

"I wanted to be a ballerina when I was little, and I am, sort of. But the reality is, I'll never be you." She shoved a handful of chips into her mouth to demonstrate.

"You're a really good dancer."

"Yeah, well, my nickname around town isn't Prodigy."

I felt myself blushing. I had a love-hate relationship with that nickname. Yeah, I'd worked my butt off to get where I was as a dancer—I even turned down *potato chips* to keep my body lean—but the name Prodigy should feel special, right? Mostly the name just felt like a disappointment. The girl I could have been before I got knocked up and had to switch my whole career around. I frowned, remembering the modifiers kids at school had whispered behind my back. Slut Prodigy. Sex Prodigy. Prego Prodigy, which didn't even make sense.

"Tell me," Peyton said. She circled her hand, as if coaxing out my secrets. There was salt on her fingers. "You're obsessing about something. Tell me now."

I shrugged. "I'm just thinking about everything."

"Don't do that. We agreed about this, remember? No bad feelings about the past. The past is behind you." Peyton leapt up, yanking me to my feet. "We cannot change the past, only live in the moment."

"Oh God."

"This moment is your destiny."

"Stop. Please." I was smiling.

She bowed, the chips accidentally spilling. "You will silence your critics by winning that scholarship and blowing them all away as Lakefield's true prodigy." She stopped flitting around when the door opened. Juliette, my dance teacher and aunt, was barefoot, her strong legs shiny with some kind of oil. The only thing country about her was the music she preferred. She gestured to the carrier. "Barbara wouldn't watch her?"

"She had plans."

Juliette didn't mention it was Danny's night to babysit, which she knew. I wasn't the only one getting used to him being busy.

"Plans that didn't include helping her daughter win the most important scholarship of her life?" Juliette leaned over the carrier handle and smiled wide at Nell. When she smacked her little lips, Juliette and Peyton both melted.

"Aw," Peyton said.

"Maybe she thinks I should add 'day care' to the sign." Juliette wasn't really mad, but she always made a point that she and Mom butted heads on the topic of my teen mom responsibilities. Juliette wanted me to be as free as possible, with support from Mom as needed.

My mother was of the opinion that Nell was my number-one priority, which she was. Her and one hundred other responsibilities. I'm pretty sure their differences had a lot to do with how their lives had turned out—Mom, a single parent of two girls; Juliette, a free spirit who owned Shining Waters, one of the most elite dance schools in the country. Mom was overwhelmed and tired from running the business end of the school, while Juliette loved life and had the body of an eighteen-year-old.

"Hey, guys," I said. The girls who had trailed in behind Juliette clustered around Nell.

"She's honestly the cutest baby I've ever seen," Monique said. The twins—Sofia and Svetlana, from a well-off family that spoke in Russian half the time—nodded as Monique dropped the one bag she'd brought to the side. One bag.

One.

She had no idea how much I envied her.

"I'll tell Barbara she cried the whole time," Juliette decided. Nell continued to sleep. "And you." My aunt pointed her French-tipped nail at me. "I'll push you twice as hard until she wakes up. We've got one month."

"I know. I'm ready to work."

"Getting accepted to Wist simply isn't enough," Peyton said. She liked to brag about me, which only made me feel weird.

"I still think you should apply," I said, but Peyton made a *nah* sound.

Wist School of the Arts. New York City.

Sometimes I felt like pinching myself. Wist was really happening. I hadn't completely ruined my life by getting pregnant.

With the grueling admissions process behind me—the live audition in Chicago followed by me begging the faculty for a one-year deferment—all I had left to worry about was how to pay for it. There was tuition, an apartment, child care on the days Danny wouldn't be able to help, dance clothes. The Leona Barrett Scholarship could pay for all of that and then some, and I'd been picked as a finalist to represent the Midwest based on my video submission and essay. Just one step and six competitors left to go. So—yes. I was definitely ready to work.

"Okay, girls. Let's go through class and then focus on your individual pieces."

We spread out in the studio, which was designed to feel like a modern retreat—good lighting, seamless wood floors, and giant black-and-white photos on the walls. Each image was a close-up: pointe-shoe ribbon strings; a dancer's hair lit by a spotlight. We warmed up as Juliette walked, toe to heel, into the center of the room. She still had those beautiful high arches, feet we were both born with, made for dance. The studio was my second-favorite place in the world, second only to being with Danny.

When the ensemble pieces were done, I caught my breath next to one of the huge windows overlooking the woods, a dancer's muse. Beneath my fingertips, the pane was cold from the recent rain. The stress of my day receded like a wave.

"I want it perfect," Juliette snipped, breezing past. So I began.
Stretching.
Bending.
Clearing my mind of everything, letting dance take over.

That unbelievable feeling of connection—that's why I danced.

As I moved over the wood floor, I felt the ache of my past pushing me.

Work harder. Pay attention.

I lost track of time, even when sweat formed at my hairline and my feet burned. Peyton jogged toward me with her hand out.

"Your phone went off."

"It's probably Danny."

I stole a tiny peek at the screen, pretending not to notice Juliette's disapproving frown from across the room.

"Is it him?" Peyton said, nudging me.

"Uh, Jen texted."

We exchanged a look. Peyton and I didn't care for Jen, who was a senior like us. She was the kind of girl you said hi to but didn't trust. I opened the message and tried to hide the instant worry I felt, fear rising from the bottom of my stomach to the back of my throat.

I heard about Danny. Are you okay?

CHAPTER 3

AARYN

Phoebe smiled and slid closer to Chaz on the marble bench in the alcove, making room for me. He didn't bother moving out of her personal space.

"Hey," I said, soft, right against her cheek.

"Hey," she said back. Cupid briefing, Dad's place, always way too early. I was on time. I leaned over my quiver with my hands clasped. Two golden arrows glinted up at me. Check and check.

"It's been a while since we've reviewed history," Dad said, silencing the group. He stood before us wearing a gold cape over his wings, wings only he, the original cupid, had grown. The wings were vintage and cool and not something I would have hidden given the choice. I squinted and read the text on the screen behind him.

THE CUPID'S PURPOSE

Stuff we'd learned in prep school.

Images of couples he had shot with arrows over thousands of years hung around him. We knew them well. Cleopatra and Mark Antony. Bonnie and Clyde. Johnny Cash and June Carter. My mother, Psyche, had been up there until she and my dad separated two years ago. Yeah. Some epic love stories don't last as long as others.

"I designed the arrows to help people. Because of us, love is a reality all over the world."

He carried on and on.

Humans no longer have to waste years of their life searching for their other half.

The arrows have changed history.

When you became a cupid, you strengthened your rank among the gods.

Humans like to believe in love.

They need love.

We make love happen.

And then Chaz raised his hand and said the one thing that got my attention all morning. "Can you speak to all the changes in technology? Because humans are connecting to their soul mates—without our help—every day."

He may as well have faced the group with an arrow pointed at us. No one moved. I'm pretty sure we all held our breath, since Chaz seemed to be reading from Tek's manifesto word for word. Tek had been a cupid like us for a while, then ditched the program to "start his own thing." He wrote a manifesto, "Sex and Human Exploration," to explain his plan.

"I've read Tek's essay," Dad said dismissively. "By the way, is that a direct quote?" His history lesson began to make sense.

"Correct me, though—I didn't see the term *soul mates* mentioned. Not once."

I glanced over at Chaz. Could he give Phoebe a little space? He knew we were a thing. We didn't have an official title, since Phoebe wasn't big on that, but everyone knew we were good together. Ever since I'd passed my final, we'd been a couple. "I'm just saying, we all know the arrows are powerful, but there are lots of ways for humans to fall in love now."

"But an arrow's forever," I said. The room got really quiet again. Phoebe hesitated, then slid her fingertips down my arm for a few seconds.

Dad nodded at me. "Exactly, Aaryn. Now, let's get to work. It's a good day for love."

The briefing adjourned just as a goddess ran into the room. A messenger goddess. One of Iris's girls. She wore the traditional white dress, silk, and made a beeline for my father, cupping her hand to his ear.

The sound of the others talking grew louder.

"Thank you," Dad murmured, which sent the messenger girl hurrying out of the room.

"What was that about?" I asked. My arrows rattled to one side.

"Just a meeting I have to go to. Something about an audit."

The set of his jaw, the storm in his eyes and the way he avoided looking into mine, the way he'd said *audit* as if it wasn't foreign or strange, and the way he strode through the door with his hands in fists, tight to his sides, paralyzed me.

The questions in my mouth were liquid. The air had cooled. When Phoebe said goodbye, not picking up on my fear, I didn't reply. Just stood still until the room emptied.

Last year I landed on Earth, invisible, and used my arrows to make two people fall in love; and then I came back. That was my story. I had to stay calm.

Dad and four guards were waiting for me in my room when I returned.

"Did you think I wouldn't find out?" Dad asked. He faced me in the stoic way he faced everyone: as the leader. His arms were crossed. This time, his wings drooped beneath the cape, and noticing them, a feeling of relief, almost like forgiveness, hit me and spread. Finally, after a year of pretending everything was fine, that I was a good son and a good heir, someone had discovered what had gone wrong that night back on Earth. But what would happen to me?

"I don't know what you're talking about," I said, stalling.

"The practice arrow? Finals?"

From there, my father's words blurred.

The assembly knows what you did.

Write down your arrow PIN.

I'm disabling it.

You're going to get a chance to fix your mistake.

"How?" I blurted out. The room was too bright, almost as if the sun was cresting the horizon, shining directly into my eyes. "How will I fix anything without an arrow?"

"I don't know. But you're going to try."

"I won't go to Blackout?"

Dad clasped his hands behind his back. "You'll have ninety days before that happens. You, and by default, Phoebe."

"What?" My legs felt weak. "Where is she?" The room was spinning. "What have you done with her?"

"She's taking a leave of absence while you're gone."

"Don't let them hurt her. She doesn't deserve any of this. Promise me." Breathe in. Breathe out.

"If you can get the guy to propose, you can come home as if nothing ever happened."

The room came into focus. "And if I fail?"

"You won't. You can't."

"But what if I do? What will happen to Phoebe?"

"I can't change the codes. You know that. I did the best I could." Dad picked up the paper with my PIN and handed it to a guard, who took it with robotic-like stealth. "Phoebe is part of this whole mess, just as much as you. But you're the one going to Earth."

Deep down, I'd been waiting for someone to find out. That's the thing about guilt. You don't want your secrets exposed, but the guilt keeps you up at night. The guilt changes who you are and throws you into a dark corner, alone. Even my flawless work ethic since finals couldn't make up for what we'd done.

My father pawed through a folder full of papers, almost as if he didn't understand what he was doing, either. "Ninety days. There's no Blackout for anyone if you can fix this."

"But how do you get someone to fall in love without an arrow?" I asked.

Dad froze for a long time before answering. The room felt humid, almost eerie, as if fog had crept down the mountain to conceal us. "There's more to love than arrows."

"Like what?"

"Here." He handed me a photo. "Her name is Karma Clark. She got pregnant. The couple—the two from that night—they have a family now." She had these pretty, deep-set big eyes and a mouth that turned up at the corners.

My father held out a second image. "Danny Bader. Get him to propose. Talk to him, reason with him, talk to the girl, too. Karma. Help him fall in love with her."

I shook my head slowly. "This isn't going to work."

"You're going to Earth as a human."

Diorthosis, the god who fixed things, stepped into the room but didn't meet my eyes. He had the features of an ornate sculpture and appeared to be chiseled from gold.

"Everything will be taken care of while you're there," Dad said, sliding another item from the folder. Bold letters were typed on the card. We'd learned in prep school about IDs and other objects humans use on Earth. Never thought I'd need them, though. "Use the name Aaryn Jones when you need help. Diorthosis will keep everything straight. He can influence humans to help you."

"To an extent," Diorthosis said.

We turned to the sound of someone running toward the door. The curtain snapped aside.

My mother. We hadn't spent much time together since she and Dad split. The fact that she was here scared me a little. Dark hair billowed around her face—her face, always a source of scorn among the goddesses; a face too beautiful, they warned, like that was a bad thing.

"Aaryn!" She hugged me.

"It's time to go," Dad said.

My mother reached to cup my face, an action that showed the golden sun tattoo on her upper arm—the mark that reminded us she was once human. "Promise me you'll try to enjoy it," Mom said. Her hand relaxed. She absently touched the tattoo. "You will feel much different than you do now, and . . . there will be so much to see and feel."

"Tell Phoebe I'll be back for her," I said.

"You're destined to be powerful," Dad said. "I know how hard you've worked to learn everything. You can do this."

One of the guards filled a syringe. It didn't resemble the needles I'd seen on Earth, clear tubes with pinprick noses. This device was made of metal, its end the size of a drinking straw. The liquid that filled its gut was thick and yellow. Mom held three fingers to her mouth and looked like she might cry.

"I love you so much," she said.

My father's grim nod was the only command needed for the syringe to be plunged through my skin. I yelled as the serum seared through my body like fire. The world exploded before my eyes.

All I could see after that was Mom's face leaning toward me, whispering, "You deserve to know the truth."

And then blackness.

»»» CHAPTER 4 «««

KARMA

"What did Jen want?"

My face must have given away my worry, because Peyton hitched her hand on her spandex-covered waist and read over my shoulder. Her face scrunched. "'I heard about Danny'?" she read. "What is *that* supposed to mean? Heard what?"

I arched my back and gave a little roll of my shoulder. "Who knows. Probably some stupid rumor." The music for my piece blasted from the speakers, but I couldn't even remember what I was supposed to be doing. Jen knew something about my boyfriend before I did. So?

I didn't care.

I didn't care so hard that suddenly it was all I could think about. Across from us Juliette was nagging Svetlana about her form.

"Call him."

I toyed with my phone. "He probably won't answer." I regretted saying that when I noticed the pitying expression on Peyton's face. "I think he's at football practice anyway."

Peyton led me across the room and out the screen door, which creaked as we snuck out, the sound of crickets sharpening. "They'll hear Nell if she wakes up." Peyton touched my elbow. "Call him. I know you want to."

The phone felt clammy in my hands. "Okay." The narrow porch seemed to spiral as I leaned against the railing, each ring rattling my brain.

Danny didn't answer. I ended the call and tried to act like I didn't care that he was ignoring me. "I'll try him after rehearsal."

"Did you reply to Jen?"

"No."

"If she ever messaged me about Nick, acting like she knew more about my boyfriend than I did—I'd flip the frick out on her." Peyton pointed at me with her eyebrows raised.

"It's probably nothing." My skin crawled with worry.

"Maybe you should call her."

"No!" I clicked the power button, but there were no new messages. "I'll stop by his house after rehearsal." I smacked a mosquito on my leg. I really had to get back inside. I didn't move.

"Okay," Peyton said. "Talk to him in person. Good. If you want, I'll take Nell home for you. You can tell me all about it when you get back."

"Thanks. I'll switch out the car seat." I smiled, but I could tell she had a bad feeling about the message.

The rest of rehearsal was agonizing.

>>- - - - →

My phone lit up as I was leaving, and for a second, my heart pounded so loud, I felt dizzy.

The air rushed out of me as I read the display. Leah. "Hey, I can't talk right now."

She was eating something loudly. Taffy, maybe. "Do you think you could pick me up a pack of smokes?"

"You shouldn't smoke."

"They're not for me, they're for Benjamin. He said if I . . . Well anyway. Pretty please? Just this once? I won't ask again, I promise."

I hit the gas and racked my brain for an image of what Benjamin, the mentioned dimwit, looked like. The way Leah switched boyfriends, it was hard to keep them all straight. "I don't supply cigarettes to minors."

"Uh-huh. Where are you going?"

I felt a headache coming on, throbbing right between my eyes. "I have to stop at Danny's."

"Tonight? Why?"

"None of your bees. Peyton is dropping Nell off. I definitely don't have time to stop at the gas station. I'm driving, so goodbye."

"Come on, Karma, please? Remember when you got pregnant and I helped you with everything, even the gross stuff?"

"Stop it."

"I really need your help."

"I'm not going to help you date losers. I heard what you were doing at that party. Making out with two guys? I'm telling Mom to put you on birth control."

"Who told you that?" For a while the only sound was my tires on the gravel road. "Did Danny say something to you?"

"It wasn't Danny," I lied. The sound of candy being unwrapped hurt my ear.

"He has no business reporting what I do. You'd think he'd try to be nice to me after everything he did. Guess not." She had her bratty-little-sister voice on. I could almost imagine the way she was blinking and bobbing her head. "Guess I shouldn't be surprised. Tell him I said to worry about himself."

"For your information, Danny and I have moved on."

"How precious."

"Good luck getting your cigarettes." I hung up.

A dark mood filled me. *Shana* hadn't meant anything to Danny, though Leah wouldn't stop reminding me about her, the one-night stand Danny had slept with a week after homecoming. He'd been beyond drunk when she threw herself at him. Leah told me to dump him immediately, but what did she know about love? Danny and I *had* moved on from him cheating, and I really, really wished she would do the same.

My screen lit up. Leah's message:

Sorry. Love you.

I rolled my eyes and wrenched the wheel, my car bouncing to a stop at the gas station.

My headlights fanned across Danny's truck in the barnyard. I liked the way the dairy farm looked at night. Peaceful. Like it hadn't witnessed the dysfunction of its owners over the years.

Judy answered the door.

"Karma, my goodnesh." Danny's barrel-chested mother

pulled me against her, the smell of farm and booze turning my stomach. Mom and Juliette had gossiped about how much she drank since her husband had died five years ago. Pete had been a mean, abusive drunk, though Danny never talked about it.

"Where'sh Nell? Ish she with you?"

I forced my mouth into a smile. "Is Danny around?" The sound of guys' voices came from the kitchen. They stopped talking when I walked in.

"Prodigy." Danny's chair scraped as he stood to kiss me, just a peck on the cheek. What a sight. Danny, his two brothers, and a couple of their friends sat around a case of beer on the table. Danny's phone lay beside it.

"Hey." I tried not to melt at the sight of his sky-blue eyes, that farm-boy chest and shoulders, his flannel shirt rolled up to his elbows. Physically he was my opposite, with hair and eyebrows the color of wheat and his suntanned skin not at all like my pale complexion. For a country girl, I spent a lot of time indoors.

"Louisiana Shtate!" Judy raised her beer, and a few of the guys said, "Cheers!"

"Ma, stop that," Danny said gently. "And it's Central Louisiana."

"Can we talk?" I said.

Danny slugged a pull from his beer and crunched the can as he followed me out. He hauled his arm back and chucked the empty toward the buzzing electric fence. It bounced off a rail, clanging into the night.

"Jen messaged me." My hand skimmed his forearm and instantly my breath caught in the back of my throat. Whenever we touched, I felt better, like all the worry and anger didn't matter.

"That's what you wanted to talk about?" he said. "A message?"

I inhaled the musky country air, catching a hint of manure from the barn, but it wasn't repulsive. It smelled like home. It smelled like the place I loved to be.

"I got accepted to Central Louisiana State University," he said.

I stared at him. His eyes glittered from the floodlight over the barn. Above the light a horde of moths and insects dove and swirled.

"On scholarship," he added. He watched me, waiting for my reaction.

"Louisiana?" He hadn't told me he'd applied to any other schools besides the tech school in New York, which he'd only planned to attend on an extremely part-time basis. He obviously hadn't thought of asking me if I would think about, even consider for a second, giving up my New York.

Our New York.

"You accepted?" He couldn't be serious. An offer was one thing. Accepting it was another. But his nod was all the sign I needed for the crashing reality to hit. Our dream wasn't our dream at all. He continued to nod, his hands shoved deep in his pockets.

"I'll even be on the football team. It's really happening, Karma."

I couldn't cancel my enrollment to Wist. No way. "Danny. What the hell?"

He sighed, as if explaining to me was such a bother, so inconvenient, when there was cold beer to drink inside.

"What do you want from me?" he said.

"I don't know—consideration? We could talk about it first? Is that too much to ask?"

His arms shot out sideways. "This is such a goddamn buzz-kill."

"I didn't even know you applied there." My voice felt small—me, one person against Danny's scholarship, while inside, the rest of the Bader family celebrated. I glanced toward the barn, thinking his father's ghost was probably leering at my discomfort. Getting Danny to return my phone calls seemed like nothing now. Keeping our family together? How about that?

"Well, I did. Josh helped me fill out the application. They loved my highlight video and the rest is history."

"What about *our* history?" I said. "Louisiana is really far. How can you be a dad that far away?"

"I don't know."

"Nell needs you."

"God, Karma, I know. Don't put your baggage on me. I'm a good dad."

My eyes stung from staring so long. "Louisiana," I said, trying to get used to the word. "Maybe there's a dance program at one of the schools around there. I'll have to check."

He studied me as if thinking very hard on what I'd said. "Yeah. Maybe."

"I'm happy for you," I said. My mouth had a sour taste. Could he say something more than *maybe*?

"Thanks. I gotta get back in. See you at school."

He turned, but I pulled him in for a hug and let my cheek rest against his neck for a long time, a safe, beloved place. "See you," I said. I clung to that promise, like seeing him tomorrow would save me.

Like it would save us.

On the way home, for the first time since I'd found out I was pregnant, I smoked a whole cigarette. There was something therapeutic about the bitter taste on my tongue . . . the sting of it in my throat and lungs. I could see why people liked smoking.

The only part that didn't feel right was the buzz. There was nothing euphoric about what I'd learned that night. Peyton was waiting, but I wasn't ready to talk. I squished the butt into the driveway and walked toward my house, feeling as if all my plans for the future had burned up, just . . .

Like.

That.

CHAPTER 5

AARYN

Day 1

My eyes snapped open, then squinted at the bright sky. Birds flew overhead. I didn't follow any particular one as they darted across my vision, frantic black specks. The sky had never seemed so far away. Bursts of song, like bells screaming, came from the trees where the birds landed.

Tap-tap. Tap-tap.

The thud of my heart.

I rolled onto my side. Blades and blades and blades of grass slid from focus. A beetle. Flickering rays of sun. I winced as something dug into my leg. I pulled a wallet out of my pocket and slid the cards out slowly: a Florida driver's license, a Social Security card, a bank card. My identity as Aaryn Jones was already in motion. My photo on the license was awful, one eye half closed, my expression lifeless.

With a sharp breath, I extended my arm and turned it in the light, my same olive skin, my same hand.

But I was human.

I froze at the sound of a girl's voice.

"I swear, I saw someone. He was—"

I stood and the four teenage girls coming my way stopped dead in their tracks. They were wearing workout clothes, and two of them were twins. We stayed like that for a while, staring the way you might at an animal you find in the woods.

"Hi," I said. I crossed my arms over my bare stomach, feeling exposed with no shirt on. "I'm Aaryn." Then I added, "Aaryn Jones." I made a quick scan of the area—lots of trees, a building, and a pond. I'd landed there for a reason. An unknown reason, but still.

"I know this sounds crazy, but can one of you tell me where I am?"

The twins had turned and started walking away. One of the two remaining girls pursed her lips. Her T-shirt said *I Live to Dance.* "Uh, yeah. We have to go." She took the other girl's arm. They didn't waste time turning around.

I stumbled to follow them. "Is this your house?"

The other girl glanced over her shoulder, her red hair pulled back in a tight ponytail that fluttered in the wind. They kept walking.

Hmm. I knew her somehow.

Oh wow.

I half tripped, then snapped off the end of a wildflower as the memory got clearer. It was her! The girl Phoebe shot—one half of the tongue-war couple.

I rounded the corner of the building. The girls were standing on the porch. "If you wouldn't mind helping me out for a min-ute." I grimaced. "I was on a hike. Got a little lost." I really wished I had a shirt.

"Wait here," said the redhead. They all went inside.

"What do you mean, you found him . . ."

A woman pushed the screen door open and let it slap against the frame behind her. She was barefoot and wearing a sundress and sunglasses. She held a half-eaten carrot in one hand.

"Can I help you?" she said. She frowned.

"Hi," I said, hoping to sound normal. "Nice place you have here."

"Yes, well, you were just caught trespassing." She whipped off her sunglasses.

"I got lost. Long hike." I held out my hand. "Aaryn Jones."

And the moment I said my name, her frown disappeared. She blinked. "Aaryn." Took my hand. "Aaryn Jones, of course." She smiled. "I had a feeling we knew each other from some-where. I'm Juliette Girard." She indicated the girls standing be-side her. "This is Peyton and Monique. Two of my students here at Shining Waters."

Both girls gaped at their teacher.

Diorthosis. "Nice to, uh, see you," I said.

"Now, how can I help you?" she said.

"I, uh, well, I don't really know why—I mean how—I ended up here, but—"

"Do you have a place to stay? How about a ride? You're a couple of miles from town, you know."

Peyton grabbed Monique's elbow. "How do you think she knows him?" she muttered.

"I lost my phone," I said, thinking fast. "Maybe you could, uh, take me to the store to get a new one?"

"You must be hungry."

"Yeah," I said.

Whoa. I shifted uncomfortably. I'd never *needed* to eat until now. Food on Mount Olympus wasn't eaten to survive—it was eaten for show, or for enjoyment.

"One of the philosophies here at Shining Waters is that we should feed our whole selves—body, mind, and spirit. If those things aren't fed, you won't be your best." Juliette pointed to the steps. "Wait here. I'll be right back."

Minutes later she returned with a huge salad and a bottle of water. She perched on the other side of the steps and finished her carrot while I ate.

"Thanks," I said, spearing a cucumber. "It's really good."

"Good." She slid her sunglasses into the neck of her dress. "Remind me where you're from?"

I had memorized my ID. "Tallahassee, Florida. That's where I went to college. And I—" I stopped for a bit so the birds could fill in the silence. "I came here to simplify my life. I'm hoping to get a job at the high school."

School would be my best bet for securing the most Danny-Karma face time. Where did they spend their days? School. It was time for Aaryn Jones to get a real job, arrows not included.

"So you wanted to leave the big city and move to a small town?" she said, helping me out.

I nodded. "Too much noise. I was lonely there."

"Well." She slid her sunglasses back on, like she didn't want me to catch the sadness in her eyes. Too late. "Sometimes we all need to start over and connect with who we really are." She cupped her hands over her knees. "I know a guy—he has a studio apartment above his bar, nothing fancy, but it's furnished. I'll take you to town. He's an old friend of mine."

"Wow. Thanks." I felt a little bit like hugging her. I knew Diorthosis was behind the scenes, making her help me—but her kindness felt real. I'd take it.

"Lakefield's a small town full of good people. You'll see."

"Thanks."

"Do you have enough cash for a security deposit?"

"A what?"

"Money for the apartment?" she said.

"No, I, uh, need to get some."

"We can swing by an ATM."

No idea what she was talking about, so I just smiled.

"Is there anything else you need?" she asked.

"Yes. There is." I cleared my throat. "How can I get this guy I know to fall in love with someone?"

"I beg your pardon?"

The air left me. Stupid. "Never mind."

Karma drove up just as we were going to leave.

Juliette waved at her, the keys rattling, then followed Karma's gaze to me, the person she was staring at through the windshield. Me, standing there shirtless, the sun going down, the privacy of the woods, four girls probably spying from the house—nothing could have prepared me for that.

The shock of meeting her eyes.

The clenching, my entire body registering that *she could see me*. It had been more than a year. My arrow had changed her life, yet she had no idea that I had once possessed the power to derail everything about her future.

Karma's eyes tightened at the edges, and she was the one who smiled first. Obligatory. Her face, that familiar face from the photograph—one side of her hair curved over her eyebrow.

The memories came fast—the way the arrow had felt, the way she'd looked at Danny after the kiss. Her following him into the truck.

"Mom's babysitting," Karma told Juliette. Guilt weighed on me, right in my chest. She could see me. She didn't know who I was, couldn't know, and yet—there was a chance to make things right. She could still be part of my first match.

"Glad she's helping," Juliette said. "This is Aaryn, by the way. I'm taking him to town. Aaryn, my niece Karma."

Karma and I said hi to each other at the same time.

Juliette ducked into the car, which sent me fumbling for the door handle. "Start class without me," she called.

Again Karma was giving me a curious look. It wasn't long before the rest of the girls came out to greet her, which seemed more like an excuse to stare and gossip about the weird guy they'd found in the back of the school.

Juliette buzzed the windows down, blasted country music, and hit the gas. Once on the road, the trees sped by, shadowed trunks, lots of green. I let them blur past.

All right.

Day one and I'd already found her. Next up was Danny. Somehow I had to get close to him. Match them. The music was loud with twang guitar, the scenery speeding, but my head felt clear.

I had to get home.

CHAPTER 6

KARMA

"Why is she giving him a ride?" I asked. Dust rose from where Juliette had gunned it down the road, a soft haze between the trees.

"She said she knows him from somewhere," Monique said. Her hair was shiny, slicked against her head and wound into a bun. "We found him outside the school just lying in the grass. He didn't have a phone, or a car, or anything."

"Seriously?"

"Juliette's acting weird," Peyton said. "Did she start smoking weed?"

"Peyton," I said.

"Well, then what is her deal?"

"Who cares if she knows him?" Monique said. "He's hot."

"Very," Svetlana said.

"So I guess the real question is—who's going to date him first?" Monique said in a singsong voice.

"Not me," I said, then immediately wondered why. They knew I had a boyfriend. Of course she didn't mean me.

"I call dibs," Svetlana said.

"Dream on," Monique said.

"What should we do until she gets back?" Sofia said. She didn't like fighting over boys. I wasn't even sure she liked boys.

"Let's watch a movie," Monique said.

I smiled, feeling tired and old. It would be nice to relax for once. "I'm going to rehearse."

The girls wandered back toward Kindred, the house with their bedrooms on the second floor, kitchen and living room beneath. Juliette had named the house in honor of her favorite book, *Anne of Green Gables*. Shining Waters, the studio, was another reference to the story. Peyton stayed with me. Stones skidded across the driveway as we crossed to the studio. She was quieter than usual and seemed to be studying me to find out what I was hiding. I wanted to tell her about last night, Louisiana, the whole thing.

And a big part of me didn't.

If I never told her, she wouldn't know how hurt I was, or how confused, or how pissed off I felt that Danny could ditch us without a second thought. He knew we belonged together. We had what every girl dreamed of—each other. A family. Love. We didn't call dibs on other people, because we had already called dibs on us.

"Danny accepted a scholarship to a school in Louisiana."

There. I said it.

"What?"

See, that's why I hadn't said anything: that look. That look she was giving me, her red hair all crazy in the setting sun, her mouth wide open like she'd just heard the most appalling news in the world. That look only deepened the hollowness inside.

I squared my shoulders. "And I'm going with him."

"Oh, Karma." The way she said it, like my mother had just died. The worst part was, it felt like losing someone. My dream was dying and I was at its bedside, helpless.

"What would *you* do?" I said. I wasn't really asking her advice as much as I was asking her to see the situation from my side. "Could you honestly be that far away from Nick for four years?"

We stood in the entrance, that big, empty floor glaring white in the center. Peyton seemed really shocked. "No. I mean, I know you want to be with him. But, Karma. New York." She pleaded the words *New York* as if she longed for the city as much as I did. "You won't have the same opportunities in Louisiana."

"But I'll have Danny. That's something."

"Did he . . . ?" She pressed her lips together.

"Did he what?" I fit my dance bag in one of the open spots under the bench, moving it around more than necessary. "You can say it, whatever it is." We sat on the inspirational cushions, my butt on *Dream big,* hers covering *Be happy.*

"Did he talk to you about this? Make plans with you? Anything?"

A flutter of panic shot across the top of my chest. "Yes. We talked last night, but I didn't want to say anything. You're the only one who knows."

"You had to drive over to his house just to get him to talk about it?"

"You said so yourself, it's better to talk about things face to face."

"I just don't want you to throw everything away if it's not going to work out."

"What do you mean?" My question echoed in the room. "Do you think we're going to break up?"

Peyton decided to lie. I'd known her too long, which really sucked at the moment, because she did the thing she always did when she lied and studied her knuckles. "No." The word was drawn out as when she didn't believe something. "I mean, I don't think so. Anything can happen. We're only in high school."

"I'm in love. You know how it feels to be in love."

Peyton shot me a desperate, understanding glance. "I know." She did know. She, of all people, did know. We were the friends who gushed about our guys and how much we loved them, and how awesome they were, and how we'd be together forever.

"Danny's a good guy." I wasn't sure why I felt the need to defend him all the time. "He really is. Please don't tell anyone else about this. I have to figure things out first."

Peyton sighed and we sat there in silence, each of us picking at our nails, our shared nervous habit. "Do you think I shouldn't go?" I held my breath. I'd still go, of course—I loved him—but if Peyton could honestly say that I should go to New York instead of follow Danny? That would be something.

"I'm not going to tell you what to do."

"Do you think I'm being stupid?"

Peyton gaped and smacked me with the *Inspire others* pillow. "I never think you're stupid."

We shared a small smile, two friends who had fallen in love with our guys on the same night. We were the friends who would lie as needed and sit next to each other on *Dream big* and *Be happy*. Why couldn't Danny be more like Nick? I squinted.

"Do you think there's a way Nick could coach Danny on how to be a better boyfriend?"

Peyton lit up. She loved talking about Nick. "Oh, Nick's too much of a guy. Do you really think Danny would go for that? Boyfriend lessons?"

"I was joking."

"Right." Peyton stood and snapped her fingers. She dragged her feet into a few familiar dance moves, then circled around and grabbed both of my hands. "We need to get out of this funk. I know just the thing."

"Hmm."

She plugged her phone into the sound system. A song from our favorite movie, *Dirty Dancing*, began to play.

"Ha!" I grinned, shaking my head.

"Come on," she urged.

I pretended to hate it but swung into the center of the room, mimicking Baby, the character from the movie with swingy hips. God, to be her, stuck on some ritzy vacation where the guy of her dreams sweeps her off her feet. Thanks to Juliette and her love of classic movies, we knew the scenes by heart.

Peyton laughed and tossed her hair just like Johnny Castle, the hot dancer guy, the love of Baby's life. She dropped to her knees playing air guitar.

"What did I tell you?" she said. "No funk allowed. Now dance for me, you sexy thing."

"Oh my God," I protested.

We met in the center, just like in the movie, and made a horrible mess imitating the parts we remembered.

Juliette walked in. "Wow." She clapped as we stopped. "I officially regret ever showing you girls that movie." She was smiling.

"You're proud we know all the parts," I said. It felt good

to mess around, like we were little kids again, best friends and dancer buds for life.

"We need to plan another Auntie Night soon," Peyton said. Her tone implied that I needed one more than usual. Auntie Night was sacred, a ritual we'd started last year that included the three of us and, after she was born, Nell. Requirements: all the big blankets spread out in Juliette's chill space, pillows, yoga pants, total comfort. We ate pepperoni pizza and watched classic movies and drank too much soda. We took turns snuggling Nell. We stayed up late.

Auntie Night did sound good.

"Why don't we talk about Auntie Night after your dance pieces are in better shape?"

I already felt exhausted, but there was no point in dwelling on the fact. The sounds of the forest, a rhythmic crick and creak, drifted through the screens. I forced a stage smile.

"Here." Juliette reached into her bag and held a photo toward me. "Look what I found. A little inspiration for you."

"Oh my God, my bangs!" The image of me at age fourteen, beaming. The memories flooded back. No one in Chicago had expected a country girl from Lakefield to advance to the New York City finals. I took the photo gently and held it toward the light. Peyton came to see, too.

"You were good that day," Juliette said. For some reason my stomach felt twisty and unsettled. She tapped the photo with a manicured nail. "This was the day I knew you were meant for big things."

I could feel Peyton looking at me, could feel that she was thinking about New York, but I didn't acknowledge it. "I can't believe it's been so long." Three years since I'd earned a scholarship to American Ballet Theatre in New York. Two years since I came back to Lakefield after my year in the city, high on New York, high on ballet. I'd been so desperate to get back. My break wasn't supposed to last long. Just enough time for Mom to save money so I could reenroll. Then I got the scholarship to go back. I'd just turned seventeen.

Then homecoming happened.

Juliette nodded slightly, a slow nod. A sad one. She remembered, too, and so did Peyton. We stood there, seeing it all in that photo, each of us remembering why I'd changed my mind about becoming a ballerina to focus on a modern dance career, which was better suited for my age. I had a baby. I had to heal. I wasn't getting any younger.

"Put on your pointe shoes," Juliette said. "For old times' sake."

A little thrill shot through me as I dug the pair of pink satin shoes from my bag. I tested the construction, which creaked in my hands, the satin frayed along the toe.

"I should order a few new pairs before the competition," I said. I wasn't practicing pointe nearly as much anymore, but I didn't want to injure myself.

Juliette propped herself against the wall. I rose into position, testing the boxes beneath my toes. Hopefully they could last a little longer.

She pressed play on the music. The sultry sounds of Lana Del Rey moaned from the speakers, violins reverberating in long chords, the sandpaper trot of drums.

I closed my eyes and sank into a deep stretch.

The floor was cool to the touch, my legs across it. My breasts smashed against my kneecaps, a tiny choke rising in my throat at the idea of going back to New York. God, I'd loved it there.

I gasped to compose myself and stood.

The desire to perform was a force pulling the tips of my fingers and strengthening my feet. My toes began to feel hot as I rolled through my pointe shoes, slow movements first, followed by fast ones that spanned the length of the room as Lana's voice murmured from the speakers.

I became completely lost in the moment, onstage, on display, and for the next hour my dance was all that mattered. My dance was me—a girl turning into a woman, a lifetime of work turning into something amazing. My dance—graceful, fluid, perfect, on point.

CHAPTER 7

AARYN

Day 2

The room Juliette had helped me rent was stuffy and dark. I stood, lifting the edge of the curtain that covered the window, a hint of stale smoke in its fibers.

A car drove by, the sedan hazy through the room's old glass. I used to envy humans with their dark homes and ceilings, so different from the endless clouds of Mount Olympus.

I pushed the curtain aside, flooding the room with light, and dressed quickly in jeans and the T-shirt Juliette's friend had lent me. The Nutty Pine Bar logo had a pine tree with crossed eyes and a mouth.

Yeah.

I left my apartment with the keys in my pocket and ran down the stairs. At the bottom of the stairwell I glanced up. I'd forgotten to lock my door, though it probably didn't matter. Standing with my hand on the exit, the stairwell felt like the only thing protecting me from reality. There was a softness to the space—the narrow hall and twenty-nine evenly spaced steps. The passage felt symbolic. To reach the bottom of those stairs was me taking action. Me fixing the past.

The grocery store was two blocks away, across the railroad tracks. Five cars were parked in the lot, and I, Son of Eros, passed through the double doors with no codes to stop me, just another guy in a store that smelled like fried chicken and doughnuts.

Food. Soap. Deodorant. A black can of body spray described as spicy, masculine, and exciting, to paraphrase the label. I tossed it into the cart and paid for it all by sliding Aaryn Jones's bank card into the machine, first the wrong way, so I had to fumble around and slide it again.

Card accepted.

"Have a nice day," the cashier said. She was the kind of girl who looked obsessed with being different: early twenties, piercings everywhere, and spiked hair dyed two bright colors. She seemed sad, though, like she wasn't getting the attention she wanted in life. I offered a smile and she smiled back, surprised almost, like she hadn't expected me to do that.

I wished there was a way to tell her I did see her. That we weren't so different, and that I knew what it was like to feel invisible. Knew the need to control something, even if it was just your hair color.

But remembering my purpose now on Earth, I walked out.

Lakefield was small. Most of the houses I ambled past on the way to the high school were run-down in some way, not terribly, but there were little things: grass that had grown too long, flower beds mixed with too many weeds, sidewalks that were cracked and uneven. The few homes whose owners obviously took pride in them were the ones that stood out.

The high school doors were locked. I pressed the white button next to the *Visitors must report to the main office* sign for three seconds. Cupped my hands to the glass. Groups of students filled the hallway. Somewhere inside, Karma and Danny were waiting for me.

I straightened when I spotted Karma. The buzz of the door seemed much louder than necessary.

I was in.

Karma and the other girls from Shining Waters were there, along with a few faces I didn't recognize.

"Hey," I said. The group fell silent. The girls switched between looking me over and looking at each other with silent questions. The scent of someone's body spray, strawberry, maybe, was strong and sort of delicious.

"You keep showing up," Karma said. She was smiling a little.

"Yeah, well, you can just call me Hermes," I joked. None of the girls laughed.

"Who?" Peyton asked. "I thought you said your name was Aaryn."

"Hermes. The god of transitions and boundaries? Uh, Greek god? Mount Olympus?" My face felt like it was on fire.

"You're funny," Monique said.

Karma wasn't listening anyway. She glanced down one hall, then the next, obviously looking for someone. The backpack in her arms looked heavy.

"Juliette told us you're all set up in your apartment," Monique added. Her hair was down, not in yesterday's tight bun, and hung in tight, shiny spirals. "Nice shirt."

"Yeah. Thanks."

"I'd love to see your place," said one of the twins. Svetlana, I thought. It was a weird statement.

"You should probably check in at the office," Peyton said. She seemed like the kind of girl who liked reminding people of things.

Danny rounded the corner.

He was with two buddies, big guys, all of them wearing Lakefield football jerseys. They walked like they owned the place, taking up the whole hall so anyone in their path had to veer out of the way.

The smile on Karma's face was impossible to miss.

"Prodigy," Danny called. He made a show of kissing her, though her backpack fell in the process and landed on her foot.

"Oh my God!" Peyton said. "Did that hurt? Watch what you're doing. She can't afford to get injured right now."

"I'm fine, Peyton." Her eyes darted between the two. "It didn't even hurt."

"Hi." I edged into the group. "I'm Aaryn."

Danny slid his hand off Karma's ass and knuckle-bumped my open palm. "Hey, dude. Danny Bader, running back." He didn't bother introducing his friends.

"Cool. I'm applying for the coaching position." I hesitated, mainly because it was a good idea and saying too much felt like I could ruin it. "Maybe we'll work together."

Danny scrunched up his nose. "There's an open position?"

"As of this weekend," I bluffed.

"Excuse me, but you forgot to check in." A woman dressed head to toe in flowers stood behind me.

"Oh, don't worry, Mrs. Bloom, we know him," Monique said.

I stuck out my hand. "I'm Aaryn Jones. I'm here about the open athletic position."

Her eyes widened behind flower-printed glasses, and the daisy dangles in her ears wobbled. "Open position? There's no open position here. If we were hiring, I'd be the first to know."

Crap. "Are you sure there isn't a job opening in the athletic department?" I drew out my words. "I saw it online." Hopefully Diorthosis hadn't bailed. Everyone around me was staring like I was crazy.

Mrs. Bloom waved to a man down the hall, her cheeks turning pink. "Excuse me, Coach Walt? Could you spare a moment to chat with this young man?" A man around her age, early forties, stomped toward us like he was attempting to crush the floor. His T-shirt was tight, his arms pumping as if they would show off his biceps better that way.

"Hey, Coach," Danny said. The two of them exchanged a knuckle bump, then Walt focused on me, arms crossed, and the buzzer went off for next period. Teens scattered down the hall. Danny left without saying goodbye to Karma. I couldn't help staring as she stood alone with her gaze on his retreating back.

She turned as if she'd sensed me watching. "See you around," she said. Her hair fell over one eye when she smiled.

"What can I do for you, young man?" Walt said.

I took his hand firmly. "Aaryn Jones."

And he would be my ticket in.

Fifteen minutes later Mrs. Bloom had printed a copy of my résumé and Walt was going over the benefit plan.

"Looks like the gods have smiled on us," Walt said, handing me some papers after reading over the résumé. "You have a very impressive background in athletics. All that's left now is your background check."

"What's that?"

"Standard procedure. We can't allow anyone to teach or coach without a background check. Fill this out and drop it off at the office. Then you'll be set."

"Oh. Of course. I'll get this in right away."

And a week later (not sure what was going on on Olympus, because really, a week?) I was on the field going over the roster with Walt.

"What's the story on him?" I said, tilting my chin at Danny. He was stretching his hamstring on grass that was spiky and too long.

"Danny Bader, running back," Walt said. "He's usually one of our starters."

I crossed my arms over my chest as Danny received the handoff, barely returning it to the line of scrimmage. He leapt up and exchanged words with the linebacker. The kid rolled his eyes and ignored him.

"Hey, Danny!" Walt said.

"Yeah, Coach?"

Walt was tapping his pen on the clipboard. "Aaryn's new in town, and since he's one of us now, I want you to show him around. Do something to give him a taste of the area, hiking or biking."

"How about fishing?" I asked. Phoebe and I had always made fun of the people we'd seen around the world trying to outsmart a fish. Now that I was human . . . it felt like something I should try. A rite of passage.

Walt scratched his chin. "Great choice. Get out on the lake, though it's not always the fish we're after, am I right? Peace of mind." He was nodding.

Danny's face was blank. "I can't tonight," he said. "I've got plans, and they're kind of important."

"I'm free tomorrow," I said. "My schedule's pretty open."

"That might work," Danny said, shrugging. "We don't have a game. Let me give you my number."

"My phone broke," I said. "I'm getting a new one, though." I hadn't thought of a non-creepy way to get back out to Juliette's, and I couldn't jeopardize my mission now. Turning up at a dance school uninvited, twice? No matter how eager Juliette would be to help, the phone would have to wait. I couldn't risk Karma labeling me a creep.

Walt tapped the play board. "We'll handle this the old-fashioned way. Danny, meet Aaryn at the office Friday after school. We clear?" Danny rolled his head in a half nod and ran off toward the team.

By the time practice ended, I'd realized something. Danny wasn't . . . talented.

After practice Walt offered to give me a tour of Lakefield High. I tried to pay attention, but all I could think about was the fishing trip and Danny's "important plans," as he called them. Was he going to see Karma after practice?

As if to answer my question, Danny and Karma were talking in the hall ahead of us.

"There she is," Walt boomed. "Lakefield's very own dance prodigy in the flesh."

His description seemed to embarrass her. Danny, on the other hand, beamed and bounced his arm to an imaginary beat.

Karma took a step away from him. "I better go so I can spend some time with Nell," she said. There was something hidden in the words, something Danny was supposed to get but clearly didn't.

"Sorry you can't come tonight, babe," Danny said. "Are you sure your ma won't babysit?"

"No." Her eyes were watery.

"You must be a pretty good dancer," I said. Jeez. Someone had to say something to make her feel good. One side of her mouth frowned.

"Yeah, I guess." She watched Danny, who was scrolling through his phone.

"Well, see you tomorrow," he said. No eye contact. Not even a kiss before he headed to the shower. I felt like banging my forehead into the wall.

I survived the rest of Walt's tour, but the interaction between Karma and Danny was bothering me. I made an excuse to leave and shoved against the exit door, the latch releasing with a hollow *thunk*.

Danny was standing at the bottom of the steps. It took me a few seconds to recognize him in the dark, but it was definitely him, leaning on the railing, a cologne fog stinging my nose as I got close.

"Hey, Danny."

"What up? Great practice."

A girl in jeans and a hoodie stood next to him. I hadn't noticed her at first. She looked up.

"Hi," she said.

I took a step down, then another. "Hey."

"I'm Jen. I saw you the other night at Country Café," she said, naming the restaurant I'd been going to every night. "Burger and fries, right?"

I nodded.

"Tonight's my night off," she said.

Danny glanced at her and smiled, and the look on his face made my stomach drop. Had he looked at Karma that way when they were together?

"We were just heading out to a party," she said. Danny clapped his hands together and stood in front of her.

"Ha! Not, like, a drinking party, just getting together with some friends." Busted. I heard him mutter, "Aaryn's the new coach," under his breath.

Jen's eyes widened. "Oh! I thought he . . . Well, never mind what I thought. We're, uh, getting together with a few friends."

A party, huh? I decided to play the part.

"It's cool. I like to party."

Danny seemed eager to trust me. "You do?"

"Yeah. Florida State, remember?" I made a drinking motion. "You can trust me."

Jen nudged him. "We should go," she whispered.

Danny stood with his arms behind his back, baseball cap barely above his eyes. "You wanna check it out?"

Jen smacked him.

"Definitely," I said, and Danny grinned.

"Awesome. You can get to know some of the guys. Ride with us. We're meeting up at Dmitri's shack. Double Ds!"

"His shack?"

"His hunting shack. It's not far."

I gave an enthusiastic thumbs-up. Jen used him to block the wind as she leaned forward to light her cigarette. Maybe they were just really good friends, like Phoebe and Chaz had been. She met my eyes for a second when the cherry burned.

Danny's phone was buzzing in his pocket.

He made no attempt to answer it.

CHAPTER 8

AARYN

Day 9

Jen hoisted herself into the middle of the truck cab, and I followed.

"Too bad Karma can't come," I said. Neither of them said anything.

The dirt road on the way to the shack was in rough shape. We bumped into each other a lot, the truck shocks bouncing, us crashing together. Us being Jen, Danny, and I. Not Karma and Danny.

Jen and Danny.

I held my arms to my sides to keep from touching her, but it was pointless. Danny spread out like he was totally in his element.

"Maybe we should invite Karma to come fishing tomorrow," I said. Jen whipped out a new cigarette and snapped the lighter.

"She's busy, man," Danny said. "Dance practice, studying."

"Maybe we could meet her at the café," I said. "Grab a bite to eat."

"I work tomorrow," Jen said, her mouth full of smoke.

"Hey, man, what are you getting at?" Danny turned to me with furrowed brows. "Do you like her or something?"

"No! I just thought—"

"Me and Karma go way back, man. She's my girl."

Jen crossed her arms and blew a giant cloud of smoke in the cab.

"I just thought you might want to spend time with her," I said, realizing with every word how lame I sounded.

"Dude. Just . . . don't."

We made a hard stop at the shack. The place was really a dump, five cars parked in no order, Christmas lights wound sporadically through the trees. The roof bowed in the middle. Danny and Jen climbed out through his side, but they weren't holding hands or anything. If Danny thought I was trying to make a move on Karma, gods help me.

I had to relax.

I opened the truck door just in time to hear a dark-haired girl on the porch greet Danny.

"Hey, loser," she said. Jen kept a good distance from him now. She didn't look back when she entered the shack.

The girl flipped the lid of a cooler and tossed an ice cube at Danny's shirt. "God, come on, get a little tipsy. Maybe then you won't have to blab reports about me to my sister." Her hand slithered over Danny's shoulder, but when her glossy eyes met mine, she shoved Danny aside. She was strong for such a small girl. "Damn, Danny, who's your friend?"

"Get lost, Leah. You're jailbait. How'd you get wasted so fast?" He handed me a beer. "Karma's little sister," he explained.

"Heeey," she said. Beer sloshed from the can she was holding. "I'm Leah."

"Hi," I said politely. God, she looked really young. Danny waved to a girl inside the shack, and I immediately began to analyze the gesture. Friendly? More than friends? I cracked the beer open.

"So, Danny's friend, how do you know Danny?"

I gave Leah a one-second look. "I'm the assistant coach for the football team. We just got done with practice." I set the beer on the porch railing.

"You're a teacher?" Leah swayed. "I have not been drinking at all, then, not a single drop."

The bad British accent she spoke in almost brought a smile to my face. Her eyes glittered and then she laughed, mouth hanging open. She fell against me a little. Girls weren't much different than goddesses when it came to getting wasted.

"I'm not really a teacher," I said. Anything to get her off me. "Just a coach."

"Coming, Aaryn?" Danny said.

Leah had lit a cigarette and positioned herself against the porch in what I assumed was supposed to be a seductive pose.

"Later, Danny's friend," she said, waving with her pinky.

I got the hell out of there.

The music volume was maxed. I'd expected to hear country, not the hip-hop that blasted; country kids using music to escape their reality. Everyone stared at me.

"This is Dmitri!" Danny shouted. The shirtless guy wearing

patched overalls slung his arm around Danny. They chanted a chorus of "Double Ds!" complete with a dance that involved them hopping from one foot to the next.

"I'm Aaryn!" I yelled in return. Dmitri spat tobacco behind him and offered me a bottle of Jack Daniel's. I took a long pull, but the sting of booze felt wrong. I had to get out of Lakefield. Phoebe needed me, and this time I couldn't let her down. If Danny got drunk, maybe I'd be able to talk to him about Karma without making him mad.

Hey, buddy, you should marry that girl!

"Where's Prodigy, man?" Dmitri said.

"Couldn't get a sitter!" All of this shared in shouts.

"What a drag, man. She never comes out anymore."

"Karma's great," Danny said. "But it's rough sometimes, you know? Being a teen dad?" He tipped the bottle up for a long time.

The door of the shack flew open.

I'm not really sure how Leah managed to fall so fast, but I heard a loud thump above the music. Her hair sprayed forward, her hands slapped against the floorboards, and then she didn't move.

"Whoa!"

The teens crowded around her, but Danny didn't get too close. I leaned down.

"Are you okay?" I asked. She lifted her head, her hand flying up to her mouth.

"Nnmokay," she mumbled. A trickle of blood ran over her knuckles. Someone killed the music and she began to cry.

"Here, sit up," I said. Dmitri tossed me a rag, and with my help Leah took it clumsily, her hand splotchy with blood.

"I'm fine," Leah said. Her dark eyes flicked toward Danny, who was swigging more booze. "Why'd you bring Jen to the party?"

"Don't start drama," Danny said.

Dmitri stepped up. "Yeah, Leah, not at my shack."

"You know what you are?" Her bloody hand was bent in Danny's direction. "You're an asshole. You and your friend." She pointed at Dmitri.

"Let's go outside," I said.

"No, I want to hear what this *asshole* has to say about why he ditched my sister so he could drink and party with another girl."

I definitely had to stop that conversation from happening. Leah clambered to her feet.

"You're wasted," Jen said. She stood by Danny, smoking. "Maybe you should just go home."

"Come on." I led Leah by the elbow. Her mascara ran in two black lines down her cheeks. "Sit on the porch. I'll be back with some water, okay?"

She shrugged my hand off and staggered down the steps into the driveway.

"Leah, wait!"

She didn't look back. Inside, Dmitri had grabbed a blond girl to dance with while Danny smacked his hands to the beat.

The sound of insects grew louder as I ran from the shack. At the car, Leah was snuffling, the crumpled rag in her hand as she fumbled with the keys. Blood splattered on the car door.

"I'm so embarrassed," she said, and actually choked a little on the blood in her mouth. "I tripped or something, I don't know. Danny's such a jerk." I helped her position the rag. Thanks to Phoebe's joyride idea during one of our assignments, I knew a little bit about how to drive a car. I placed one hand on the car door and reached for the keys with the other.

"Give me those," I said. "Let me drive you home."

CHAPTER 9

KARMA

I peeked out the front door with Nell balanced on my hip. Who was that with Leah? I stole onto the cold concrete and blinked into the darkness.

Aaryn's deep voice directed Leah. "Watch out for that rock." Patient. "You're sure this is the right house?" Sultry and smooth. The kind of voice that would be perfect for audiobooks. A voice to be alone with. Svetlana would die when I told her he'd been at my house.

"Leah?" I clutched Nell tight. "What happened to you? Are you bleeding?"

"Is Mom home?"

"Oh my God, there's blood all over your chin."

Aaryn stood behind her with his arms crossed. He was wearing a fitted black T-shirt and jeans. I pulled my sister under the porch light. "Tell me what happened. Did someone hurt you?" I exhaled against the top of Nell's head. "You reek of cigarettes and beer."

"Where's Mom?"

"She's shopping in Medford."

Leah hugged me. "Everyone saw me. The music stopped and everything."

"Saw what? What happened?" I rubbed her back as Nell grabbed a handful of her hair.

"I fell," she said.

"How?"

"I'm clumsy. I drank too much beer?"

"You said you were going to watch movies with your friend," I said. Aaryn studied us like he wasn't sure what he should do next. My stomach flipped. I sighed and gave my sister a squeeze. "Let's get you cleaned up. Come on in, Aaryn." *What?* I don't know what possessed me to invite him in. It just came out.

"Whose party were you at?" My voice wavered as Aaryn followed us inside. Seriously, she was going to get herself killed. I switched Nell to the other hip and thrust a handful of wet paper towels at my sister. "I thought you were done with all that trouble."

"It smells good in here," Leah mumbled. The chocolate chip cookies I'd baked—Danny's favorite—cooled on the counter, my open social studies book beside them. I'd been studying between batches. Social studies: still the most pointless course in the history of high school. The tests were so hard, all those names and dates, made worse by lack of sleep.

I had to review those chapters before the night was over.

"Help yourself." I nodded to Aaryn. "You can have one, too."

It was weird having a guy in the house. The lavender walls, the lace curtains, Mom's eggplant-colored sofa. He held his elbow as he stood next to the lamp with the jeweled fringe.

Leah chewed slowly. "I saw Danny."

"Okay. So you were at Dmitri's."

Aaryn bit into his cookie and smiled. "You made this?"

"Yes," I said. "My wild Thursday-night plans."

"But—how?"

"Just followed the recipe," I said. "Added a little love."

"Recipe?"

Leah and I watched him for a couple of seconds before he said, "Oh. Recipe. Anyway, they're really good."

"They're for Danny. It's our one-year anniversary tomorrow."

"He brought Jen to the party," Leah said. She pushed her cookie aside on the place mat.

"Jen who?" When my heart sped up, I pretended to be very busy fixing Nell's shirt, which was always riding up above her baby stomach.

"Jen from your class, the only Jen we know. Did he tell you they were going together? He didn't, did he?"

I held my sister's gaze. "I'm not getting into this with you."

"I don't think they expected me to be there."

"You shouldn't have been there, that's why."

Aaryn picked up another cookie without asking. What was he thinking of my life? My living room? The baby bouncer, the swing, the bottles I hadn't had a chance to wash? I fit Nell into her swing, but she squirmed angrily. I jabbed the power button for the music. Electronic violins, some kind of reggae beat, played over the sound of the swing gears. "Did you say anything to him?" I didn't want to seem like I was pumping her for information.

I wanted to ask her so bad.

"I called him an asshole," Leah said, quite proud of the fact. "I told him he shouldn't be at a party with another girl while you're at home taking care of Nell."

"He's just trying to have a life." My throat felt really dry. "What do you think, Aaryn?"

His eyebrows shot up. A few cookie crumbs fell from his lips. "Me?"

"What do you think about Danny going to a party with another girl? A friend, maybe? Someone he's grown up with?"

"Oh, uh . . . I'm the one who invited Jen to the party." He paused and grabbed a third cookie fast. "Not Danny. We rode in his truck, though."

Thank God. I faced my sister with my hands on my hips. "All that drama for nothing."

Leah's eyes narrowed. "Why didn't Danny tell me that? I called him out on it, and he acted so stupid."

Aaryn finished the cookie, holding the tip of his thumb in his mouth. "I wasn't really paying attention."

Leah grabbed an ice pack from the freezer and held it against one half of her mouth. "Megan told me he was saying how hard it is to be a teen dad. Give me a break. Real hard, talking about it at drinking parties."

Nell started to cry, a nasally, coughing kind of cry, which usually meant she was really tired. "He does the best he can."

"It's like you're not even dating him anymore, you're like, life-following. You follow whatever he wants, and he *does* whatever he wants. I'm sick of seeing him at parties. All I can think about is how he shouldn't be there. He should be home with you."

I sighed, so, so tired of this conversation and of worrying.

I hadn't told her about Louisiana, but she was acting like she knew. Life-following. I stopped the swing. Nell smiled at me.

"You don't get it," I said. She wasn't thinking about all the good times Danny and I had shared. The school dances, the dates when it was just us two, and our double dates with Peyton and Nick. "But I guess I do hope that he's not giving Jen a ride home. They're not that great of friends."

"Right, while you're sitting here with a kitchen full of his favorite cookies," Leah said.

Aaryn inched toward a fourth—yes, fourth—cookie.

"Hey—save some for Danny," I said.

"Sorry. They're just really good." Nell cooed for his attention and he grinned. "She looks a lot like you."

My little babe. I picked her up and kissed her cheek, bringing her closer to him. She tried to whack him with her fist.

"Can I hold her?"

I shrugged. "Sure."

I fit Nell into his hands. She was wide-eyed and excited, pounding him with both fists. His chest appeared solid enough for the beating. "Hi, sweetie," he said, and Nell answered with her adorable baby talk, cute enough to make me think it had all been worth it.

Then she puked.

"Oh my God." I grabbed her burp rag as Leah snorted, and began to wipe the white stain on his shirt. The fabric puckered where the liquid sank in. "I'm so sorry. That's probably why she was crying."

Aaryn held Nell at arm's length, like he was afraid she might do it again. "Wow. That's a first."

Smiling, I gathered her up and cradled her. Funny how

shocking puke could be when it wasn't part of your everyday routine.

"Oh well, a little puke never killed anyone, right?" he said.

I aimed and tossed the rag at his chest.

"Hey!" He dodged that thing pretty fast.

"How old are you?" Leah asked. Great, now she was interested in him. I knew my sister too well.

"Nineteen." He picked at his shirt to help it dry. "Hey, Karma, did you know I'm going fishing with Danny tomorrow?"

"Oh?" I filled a bottle with water, then shook the formula out.

"Yeah." Aaryn sat on one of the stools behind the kitchen island, the one with the ruffled vinyl edge. "I told him to invite you to the café after, but I think he took it the wrong way. He got kind of jealous."

My face flushed at the thought. Danny, jealous of Aaryn? "Really? Well, tell him I said sure. That would be nice." I smoothed Nell's hair from her ear to her neck with my fingertip. Silky and soft, so precious. "I mean, it's our anniversary, so it would be nice to get some extra time together."

"Is he normally a pretty jealous guy?"

"Danny? Oh no, not really. I don't know."

Aaryn clapped his hand to his forehead. "Duh—I guess he'd rather hang out with you instead of fishing. Not too romantic if I'm there. I'll cancel."

"No, no, no, it's okay, really. You don't have to cancel. I have dance and homework, and it's not like we have a sitter." Nell squirmed when I hugged her. "Do you want to see what I got him?"

"The suspense is killing me," Leah said.

"Yes," Aaryn said.

It wasn't until I was at my bedroom door that I realized he'd followed me. "Oh, uh, you can just wait in the kitchen." But the door opened when Nell banged on it, and he saw the mess, my God, how embarrassing. Thankfully the path to Nell's crib and her neat pile of belongings looked somewhat responsible.

"You weren't supposed to see that," I said, flipping on the light. I really had to make it a priority to clean my room.

"I mean, who could expect that your clothes would, you know, go *into* the basket instead of onto the floor?" Aaryn said.

"Shut up. I have bad aim. And bad rebound." I found Danny's gift among the clutter without any problem.

"Here it is. Cute, right?" The photo frame had three images. "This one's from homecoming, the day I knew he was my Mr. Right." I wore a pink dress; he, a suit coat and baseball cap. Aaryn's smile had changed to a weird half gape. "I was so nervous," I said, and let out a weird, three-second giggle, almost like I was there again. Maybe my nerves had something to do with how crowded the hall felt with Aaryn next to me. He seemed comfortable standing inches away. "I guess this one speaks for itself." The shot of me and Danny, him giving my belly a thumbs-up—classic. Nell kept trying to grab the frame. "So yeah. That's his gift."

" 'You're my everything,' " he read aloud, which is what I'd doodled across the final photo, one of me taken during a dance shoot.

"Is it dumb?" I cradled the frame against my chest, feeling insecure from the intense look he was giving me.

"Not at all." He nodded, urging me to show him again, one finger on the corner of the frame. "That pose is amazing."

"Oh, thanks. Juliette's a nag about angles. I hope Danny likes it."

"Me too." Nell beat his shoulder. "I really don't want to take up all his time tomorrow. Maybe you two can make plans."

"Maybe." I felt jumpy from all the questions I wanted to ask. "Anyway, are you and Jen dating, then? You just moved here, right? The girls told me about the hike."

Aaryn cleared his throat. "I'm not seeing anyone right now."

My pulse was erratic from the stress of Leah, the Jen thing. Lots of things. "Oh. Okay." I tapped Nell's diaper. The reggae music on her swing was still on, so I wound my way through the room and turned it off. Maybe Danny would leave the party early if I asked. It would be really good to see him, maybe just sit on the couch and watch a movie while I finished my homework. Something.

"I'm going to bed before Mom gets home," Leah said. Aaryn took this as his cue to leave.

"Yeah, well, great," he said. "Glad you got home okay." He stood in the entry with lace curtains framing him. The puke stain had dried into a crusty smear. He extended his hand and my heart did a leap. "Here're the keys."

"Oh, of course, thank you."

Leah waved and made her way to the bathroom. After a second of hesitation, I walked over. Even though he smelled like smoke, I felt relaxed around him. He had an honest face, like he wouldn't bullshit me. His gaze was direct. Curious. "Thanks for tonight," I said. "I'm glad you were at the party to help Leah. She's annoying, but I love her."

"I know." He reached for the door. Nell was punching me, eyes glued to his face. She found him very intriguing. "It's good to see you again, Karma."

He left before I could find my voice. I shivered. The dead bolt clipped in place, me with my eyes closed, inhaling Nell's scent in long, even breaths.

He was the one who invited Jen.

With a satisfied nod, I messaged Danny. He'd probably want to ditch that stupid party and be with his girls. He loved my chocolate chip cookies.

CHAPTER 10

AARYN

Day 10

"Ready to catch some fish?" Danny said. There was no hint of enthusiasm in his voice. He had dark circles under his eyes and a scrape on his jaw.

"Oh, we're still on?"

"Yeah, why wouldn't we be?"

"Uh, no reason. I'm ready." I had a new plan—make that a very necessary plan—after his near freak-out over me "liking Karma" the night before. First part of the new plan? I had to stay cool. So far, me leaning against the wall with an open copy of *Fight Club*, not at all wondering if Karma might meander by? Check and check.

"Before I forget—you were great at practice yesterday."

"You think so?"

I clapped his shoulder. "Definitely. You had some nice

moves out there. Best I've seen in a while. I told Walt he has to start you next game."

He grinned. "Awesome. Thanks, man."

When Karma rounded the corner, his mouth went straight. I pretended to be very interested in the view outside.

"Hey, guys."

"Oh, hey," Danny said. "We were just heading out."

"Do you guys have plans after?" Her question seemed rehearsed.

I could feel her gaze on me as I held the door for them, standing well out of the way. Definitely no eye contact as she passed. The fact that she smelled so good? Well. Nothing I could do about that.

"I might go to Dmitri's and do some homework," Danny said. He was acting weird, stiff-walking, his chest sticking out. "Why, what's up?"

"Oh, nothing. I might have some free time later if you want to do something. I miss you."

Her eyes had shadows under them, like his, her hair in a messy ponytail. Not that I, you know, noticed.

Danny sighed. "I'm pretty beat. I got this fishing thing now. A bunch of homework."

Karma waved her hand. "Don't worry about it." She smiled, shaking her head. "Nell woke up twice last night, little turd. I barely slept."

"Tell me about it," Danny said. "I was at the party until three."

"Did you have fun?"

"We can skip fishing if you guys want to hang out," I said. Danny blinked, gaze all shifty.

"We better get to the lake," he said.

"Yeah, okay." Karma's voice was soft. She seemed to be trying really hard not to let the conversation—or the Jen thing last night—bother her. "See you around."

She waved and the bracelet on her arm slid down, simple beads with Nell's initial dangling in gold.

His truck reeked of smoke. I'd barely shut the door when he blasted out of the school parking lot, hip-hop rattling on the speakers. We almost died on the way there. Twice. Apparently he wanted to prove he was the world's worst driver with the world's worst sound system. I sat without taking off my seat belt or talking when we arrived. Ahead of us the water was sparkling in the sun, really bright.

"Grab the bait," Danny said, two poles in hand, marching to the aluminum boat that lay on the bank. He wasn't treating me like a coach.

"Bait?" I slammed the door.

"The bucket."

The breeze felt good, like it might help me think straight. A jagged row of old, tall pine trees reflected along the back of the lake, blue sky and clouds on the rest. Peaceful. The opposite of what I was feeling. I gripped the metal handle.

Danny flipped the boat by himself. "Pick up that side."

Sand scraped the bottom and then water churned as the boat cut through the lake's surface. I jumped in and grabbed the edges as he rowed toward a patch of lily pads, feeling like I should be more relaxed. More focused. We were alone, stuck on a boat, and fishing was going to take some time.

Danny spit into the lake. Within seconds, the white spot disappeared.

"Was that a fish?" I asked.

"Yep."

"Wow." I sighed and picked up one of the fishing rods, holding it out. Phoebe would have hated the lake. Not enough going on. "So. Long night at the shack?"

Danny wiped his face with his arm, hesitating with the oars skimming the surface. "You missed a good time." He grinned and dug in the oars. "We went skinny-dipping."

"What's skinny-dipping?"

"Seriously?"

"Yeah, I . . . uh, never mind."

"Chicks getting naked, man."

The water danced. "And then what?" I asked.

"Nothing, really. Everyone was wasted. Good time, though."

"Just so you know, I never meant to sound interested in your girl."

"Hey, man, it's cool. I'm used to guys checking her out. Doesn't really bother me."

"It's just that—I had a girl like her once." I rested my arm across my knee. I was thinking of Phoebe. "Yeah, my girl was special, but we were young, too young, probably. Losing her was the biggest mistake of my life." I hadn't even said goodbye.

We'd stopped in the water, the boat sounding hollow as he placed the oars along the bottom. "You're still pretty young," he said.

"Yeah, I know, but I'm just saying—you can't let a girl like that get away." I cringed at how corny I sounded. What I wouldn't give now for an arrow, the right arrow. Shoot him and be done with it. My face felt hot.

"She's probably not too happy with me today," he said.

"Oh? She seemed okay."

"She's always on my case, man, thinking I hide shit. It's like I can't breathe without running it by her first."

"My girl was like that, too." She was nothing like that. Sometimes I wondered if Phoebe had liked me as much as I liked her. If she'd planned her days around me the way I did her.

Danny stared at the water. "Yeah." He grunted. "We'll see how college goes."

"What do you mean?"

"I'm going to Central Louisiana State University in the fall. I got a scholarship."

I tried to act cool, which equated to me sitting up with too-wide eyes. "What about Karma?"

"I think she's planning to go to Wist. I don't know."

"Wist?"

"This stuck-up art school in New York."

"Oh, you'll be long-distance, then." I almost added, *right?* "But, uh, what about Nell? Won't it be hard to live that far away?"

"Look, man, this really isn't your problem."

The understatement of the millennium. He handed me a small gray bait fish. I slid the hook through its head, like he had. Any thought of them staying together seemed far from his mind.

"I guess I thought you two were close to getting married or something."

"Married?" Danny wound the line until a tiny steel knob drew up to the tip. "We're seniors! Are you serious?"

I shrugged, the end of my line jangling. "You guys seem good together."

He flicked his fishing pole. The string settled slowly over the water. "I don't want to get married for a long time."

I'd begun to sweat. "Why not?"

"Just forget it, man."

"If you don't want to marry her . . . and you're going to Louisiana . . . then why are you together?" Marry her, all right? Get obsessed with her. She seemed pretty awesome, but what did I know? The brightness of the lake annoyed me.

"She's my girl, man. We have a kid together." He began to circle the lever on his reel. "If things go bad between us, believe me, child support would be a real drag." He frowned and threw the hook out a second time, a zipping sound.

"Okay—wait, what's child support?"

Danny scoffed. When he noticed I was serious, he frowned. "The government making me pay to support Nell, way more than I already do. The percentages are insane."

"Okay, so you *should* get married, then. Avoid all that." My hands were extended, palms up.

He made a face. "Are you gonna cast?"

Child support savings, the occasional ass grab—his perfect relationship? "Cast?" I said.

He wagged his hands, as if that helped. I stared at the contraption before me. An image of me cracking the reel into pieces flashed in my head.

I stood and copied what Danny had done, hard, but when I flicked my hands, the pole went flying and landed into the lake with a loud *dunk*. Ripples spread from the spot. I stood, and with a grunt, I jumped into the lake. For a second, the water felt good, really good, and then Danny started to yell.

"Hey! What the hell are you doing?"

All I had to do was grab the fishing pole.

I hadn't expected the water to be so cold. I hadn't expected to begin sinking. I wasn't a god anymore, and that day in the lake I faced the reality that *I could die,* right there, before getting Phoebe or Karma or myself out of this mess.

With him watching.

I didn't know how to swim, but I could claw, and kick, and try to save myself. Foam sped toward the surface, dark water all around me. Thrashing. Twisting. Nothing helped.

The sound of Danny jumping in should have been a relief, but I didn't want him to be the one to save me. He grabbed my shirt.

We burst through the surface.

"I'm fine," I said. Coughing, snorting, I tried to act cool.

"Grab the life vest, man." Water sprayed in my eyes when he threw it. I couldn't look at him. I couldn't say thank you, I owe you one, nothing. I couldn't stop feeling angry, this proud anger I wasn't even sure why I felt.

He shook his head. "That was an expensive pole, too. You got three hundred bucks?"

I clambered into the boat, breathing hard. "Don't worry. You'll get your money."

He'd saved my life. Pretty sure my dignity was somewhere in the lake, not just his overpriced pole. And the truth about what my arrow had done? I was practically drowning in it. He didn't want Karma. He didn't want to be a dad. He just wanted to be what he already was—a teenager with no responsibilities. The kind of guy who went skinny-dipping without a second thought.

It was a sad story. For Karma to love someone that much—and work that hard—for nothing.

I ripped my soaked T-shirt over my head and wrung it out. The water had a slight mineral scent. Two more truths. One: he didn't deserve her.

The second truth was a lot harder to admit, since there was no hope with her being under the arrow's spell. Danny was her everything, except what she deserved.

An eagle with a white tail and head and a black body coasted from a pine across the water's surface. I watched it as dread filled me.

She deserved to be loved.

CHAPTER 11

KARMA

"So . . . you and Danny talked about everything, then?"

The moment Jen spoke, I could have sliced the tension between us with one of the butter knives she was wrapping with paper napkins at work. We hadn't discussed Danny's scholarship at school. We hadn't discussed Thursday's party. Yet here we were, Saturday morning at Country Café, me waiting for Danny's to-go order, her with a heaping basket of silverware. How much longer could a double cheeseburger take?

"Yes," I said. "We talked." I meandered over to the bulletin board where locals stuck copies of their business cards, reading each one.

"I'm really sorry about . . ." Jen trailed off. Wrap, wrap, wrap. "About what?"

I turned to stare at her. She had these full lips—pretty, I guess, but they were dry and ugly-looking when she pursed them like that.

"Sorry about everything," Jen continued. "Wist. Plans changing." Her brown ponytail bobbed with each word. "I really thought you were going to do it this time. You know, go to New York."

This time.

Her little jabs about my past weren't going unnoticed.

"You don't have to be sorry," I said carefully. I hugged the sweatshirt I was wearing. "I've decided to go to school near Louisiana. I found a really good school." The parts I left out: an okay school; a school nearby, as in Mississippi, two and a half hours from Danny's campus. "Who knows what the future will bring? Maybe we'll all go to New York in a year or two."

Her expression was smooth, no reaction to my words. "I thought you'd be pissed."

The café was empty and suddenly too big and convenient for the topic. She grabbed a handful of silverware, the metal dinging sharply.

"I know *I'd* be pissed if my baby's father enrolled in a school ten states away without talking to me about it."

"He got a big scholarship," I mumbled.

Her mouth parted slightly, a fork in one hand, napkin in the other.

"Is *that* how he put it?"

Her words seemed to stab me. I hated that once again, she was acting as if she knew a secret, my boyfriend's secret, some members-only club I hadn't joined.

"What do you mean?" I said.

"Nothing," she said quickly.

"Jen . . ."

"Seriously, it's nothing. You worry too much." She made

a snapping sound with her tongue and something in me snapped, too.

I faced her with a pounding heart. "Yeah, well, maybe I should worry. Maybe I *should* worry that you're talking to my boyfriend and going to parties with my boyfriend when it's obvious you're not my friend." I towered over her, my fingertips supporting me on the vinyl countertop. I tried to breathe normally. I hated her lips.

"Danny wanted me to go. I can't control what he says."

"I thought Aaryn invited you."

"Who?" She fit her mouth around the straw in her water glass and took a long pull. "Oh. Him. Yeah, he was there, but we asked him to come along. Not the other way around."

I stood there for a long time. The motor for the pie display whirred, one piece of apple the only slice left. The chair grated as Jen got up and walked to the bathroom. The door closed with a gentle click.

Follow her. Don't let her make you feel small.

But I couldn't. I couldn't cross the line she'd drawn, even if it meant knowing.

To know felt like the worst thing ever, and things between me and Danny were okay again. Barely okay. I guess he'd acted a little weird when I told him about the Mississippi idea. I smiled shakily as the cook handed me a to-go container and paid for the burger, my hands trembling.

Is that how he put it?

I burst through the door of the restaurant with a snap. Shoved the burger on the passenger seat of my car and slammed the door. The crash of the river was like static in my ears. Lakefield Dam was at the bottom of the hill behind the café, inviting me to escape. I walked toward it with heavy steps, unzipping my sweatshirt as if freeing shackles, following the sound, feeling dizzy. My eyes watered from the sunlight. They stung. I could leave Jen's words at the river, pushing them out and down and gone.

Over the years, the dam had become a canvas for angst-ridden teens. Foam streaked the edges of the bank. I felt like spray-painting my own thoughts on the concrete, thinking *Jen is a bitch* would fit in perfectly between *Love sucks* and the anarchy symbol.

Her words stuck to me like paint.

I really thought you were going to do it this time. You know, go to New York.

No one understood love. If they did, they'd realize Danny and I had to stay together. Yes, I loved New York, and I loved dancing, but the desire to stay with him was always stronger. So strong I didn't understand it. Sometimes nothing I felt made sense.

But he was stupid, my boyfriend, inviting her to a party. I squeezed the locket around my neck, the one he'd given me, and pulled. The chain wasn't hard to break, a moment of the metal digging into my neck. I threw the necklace as hard as I could into the river, the gold reflecting the sun.

A second later, I ran into the water, skimming the river bottom. I lost my balance and fell forward, catching myself on a sharp rock. Blood oozed from the cut. Stupid. Stupid. I cried out and sucked the end of my finger.

"Are you okay?"

Aaryn stood on the bank, the sun highlighting every detail of him. His olive-toned skin. Black hair and short sideburns that angled an inch below each earlobe.

"No." A chill raced up my arm. "I lost my necklace." And then I grimaced, feeling embarrassed. My shoulders sagged.

"I think it landed over here." He stepped in ahead of me, dipped into the current and held out my necklace, water rolling down his hand. "Found it."

"Oh! Thank you." Water sloshed as I fumbled to take it and the locket nearly fell again, but his reflexes were good. He cupped my hand from underneath. We stood like that for a few seconds, his palm supporting mine, slippery with river but warm to the touch. Up close he had blue eyes, and there was a slight crease at each corner when he smiled. A dark freckle, one spot, marked the right corner.

His hand fell away.

"I can't believe you found it," I said. The river churned around our feet. Downstream the tan water turned blinding white as the sun hit it. "How are you, by the way? Danny told me about the lake. That must have been so scary."

Aaryn trudged to the bank. "I'm fine." He stared at the long grass, which was matted by our footsteps. "Totally fine."

"I'm glad you're both okay."

He held out his hand. I took it, and he drew me up the hill a couple of steps.

"Hey, did Danny come over last night? On your anniversary?"

"Oh, it got to be too late." I waved my hand. "I was writing a report, so it worked out fine."

"Sorry," Aaryn said. "He . . . should have stopped by."

My eyebrow raised. "*You're* sorry?" I shook my head and tried to make my laugh sound real. "You don't have anything to apologize for."

"I just feel bad that he was with me when he could have been with you. Should have been."

"Why did you lie to me?" My voice came out in a rush.

"Lie to you?"

"You said you invited Jen to the party."

"Oh." He shifted from one foot to the other.

"Danny was the one who invited her, wasn't he?"

"I honestly don't know. I found them together. You just seemed so upset, and then you said it was your anniversary the next day, and—I don't know."

"So you thought lying would make me feel better?"

"It's hard to explain."

Pine trees grew along the riverbank, hundreds of them. I was tired of seeing the same kind of trees. Aaryn reached for the necklace in my hand. The chain itself hadn't broken, though the clasp was stuck wide open. He gestured for me to turn around.

"Why'd you throw your locket into the river?" he asked. I bowed away from the sound of his voice in my ear.

He fastened it around my neck, fingertips brushing my skin. I had ripped it off on impulse, the way I'd done too many things in the past year, making a fool of myself. I could add Aaryn to the list of people who'd gotten to see the real Karma, the dance prodigy who couldn't help spinning out of control if the circumstance allowed. I was a lot like the necklace. Flying through the air, not knowing where I'd land.

"It's complicated. And stupid."

"I can handle complicated."

I hugged myself and shook my head, blinded for a second by the sun. "I better get going. Danny is probably wondering where I am." A panicky feeling rose in my stomach as I imagined asking him about the party. He wasn't a morning person. Maybe I shouldn't.

"Can I walk with you?"

"It's a free country." A cliché I hated.

"Free country?" He turned on his foot with one eyebrow up.

"Yeah. You know." I shrugged. His face tipped a little, waiting for my answer. "Uh, America?"

"Oh." He chuckled loudly, then cleared his throat. "Right. 'Free country.'" He made air quotes.

We walked toward the parking lot in silence, not the kind of silence that pressed against my chest but a safe, expanding silence. We were practically strangers—the word *strange* fit him pretty well at times—but being with him didn't feel awkward.

"I shouldn't have lied," he said. He shook his head. "You deserve better than that."

"Oh, it's okay. Seriously, I'm over it."

At my car, we looked at each other for a while, and for a second I wished he'd hug me, the way little kids are supposed to say sorry, which had to be the most stupid thing on top of all the other stupid things.

"Bye, Karma."

When he was gone I called Peyton.

We decided an emergency Auntie Night was a must. I drove to Shining Waters after dropping off Danny's burger—he hadn't felt good enough to eat it—and Peyton came outside to get Nell; she was wearing yoga pants and one of Nick's baggy T-shirts. Her hair was a mess. She hugged me. "I can't believe Jen said all that." Nell was really happy to see her, clutching the shirt, hands all over her face. "Talk about passive-aggressive," she mumbled, because Nell was gripping her bottom lip.

"I'm so sick of being lied to and explained to and ditched." I grabbed my three bags and slammed the car door. "I tried talking to Danny, but he didn't feel good."

"Oh, whatever. You deserve to know what's going on. What the hell? What is going on? How weird is it that Aaryn would lie for him? How weird is it that Danny would go anywhere with *her*?"

It felt so good to have Peyton on my side. Also, judging by the look on her face, frightening.

"I don't want Juliette to hear any of this," I said. I held my phone.

"Okay."

The morning had been awful, with Jen being such a bitch and Danny barely thanking me for the food. Me feeling weird about Aaryn. But I was safe again. I was loved.

We sat on the porch steps as I scrolled for his contact.

"Put it on speaker," Peyton whispered, then snuggled Nell to see if she was in a noisy mood. Danny didn't answer his cell phone. I hesitated, then called him at home.

My response to his mother's answer felt all too familiar.

"Oh, he's not home?"

"He went somewhere with Dmitri a little while after you left." Judy was the type of mother who hadn't taught her sons not to spit in public or lie. Yet when they needed her she had the ferocity of a mother bear. "He's been busy." Her voice had a tinny sound through the phone.

Peyton rolled her eyes and shook her head.

I angled the phone close to my mouth. "Do you know when he'll be back?"

"He didn't tell me." She clucked her tongue. "Oh, honey, is something wrong? You don't sound like yourself."

"I really need to talk to him."

She paused. "He's not gonna get away with avoiding you. We can't let him."

Mother Bear had taken my side. I smiled and shifted on the step, giving Peyton a satisfied nod. "Did he tell you I'm going to apply for the dance program at Southern Miss? We'll still be able to see each other every weekend."

"Hmm. Danny loves you girls."

Peyton may have rolled her eyes again, but I pretended not to notice. "Hopefully I'll get that scholarship. Danny said he would help me with my performance, but—"

The sound of a cellophane bag being torn open rustled loudly in the background. "You've got savings, don'tcha?"

I sat up, the step hard beneath me. "A little."

"What about your mom? Doesn't she have some sort of college fund set up for you girls?"

It seemed like an odd question coming from a mother who didn't have anything like that set aside for her children.

"I have to pay my own way." Was she really on my side? "Hopefully Danny can help out with money this summer," I added. Peyton nudged me, grinning.

"He'll be eighteen in May. It would be hard for him to keep up with his football training if he had to get a full-time job. Are you thinking you're going to file for child support?"

"Oh! I didn't mean that. No. I meant he could get something part-time, you know, just to help with some of the bills, help us save." I swallowed and focused on the group of birds clustered in the tree across the yard. They were eating some kind of seed from the pods.

Judy bark-laughed. "He has to save up for *his own* college, ya know."

"But he already got that scholarship."

"A one-thousand-dollar scholarship? Really, honey, you think that's going to cover college?"

My heart pounded. One thousand dollars? That was all? Peyton's mouth hitched open. I stood and clicked off speaker as I tromped down the stairs. The phone against my cheek felt sticky. "I thought . . . He made it sound like it was a big scholarship." I slid my hand across the hood of my car for support. Birds chirped from the trees. "It's only a thousand dollars?"

"Better than nothing."

"Oh." I inhaled sharply. Mama Bear's tone was scaring me. "Then it makes even more sense for him to get a job. He could start looking for a job now, maybe find something that's a couple of hours a week." I could hardly believe myself. I could almost picture her nostrils splayed, a fake smile on her face. Mama Bear probably wanted to paw me dead.

"Well, I'll tell him you called."

"Thanks."

"Take care, okay?"

I closed my eyes as she disconnected.

I had to confront Danny.

"We should make a list." Peyton rolled onto her stomach, picking through trail mix for the chocolate. It was late. She was lying on one end of the sectional, me on the other. Our heads met in the middle. The TV was the only light in the room. "A list of pros and cons. If the pros side is longer than the cons, you should stay together. If not—"

I felt nauseated. Nell had fallen asleep hours ago, and Juliette had gone to bed. I rubbed my stomach.

"Have you ever made a list like that for Nick?"

"No. But I have for other guys."

Why did it feel so horrible, so awful, like she was more in love than me? Why did my stomach hurt?

"I don't think I want to break up with him."

"Let's make a list."

She clicked the lamp on and found a piece of scrap paper. She pushed that and a pen across the cushion.

After sighing, I started the list, pros first.

Nice
Cute
Close to his family
A good dad
Good kisser
Good friend
Hard worker
Likes having fun

I stopped. "This is too easy."

"You haven't gotten to the cons side yet."

I added five more things to the pros side and drew a line down the middle of the page. All right. Cons.

And my eyes filled with tears. The words burned as I wrote. I worked my way down in slow, careful letters.

Avoids me

Peyton crawled over and put her arm around me. The bullet points felt a little like real bullets.

Asks other girls to parties

I shook my head and wrote again.

Cheated on me

I added, *once*. I squirmed away from Peyton, feeling fever-ish, feeling, I don't know, crazy. "I don't want to break up with him."

"Don't you want to be happy? I hate seeing you like this."

"Yes. I'm happy with Danny."

"Are you really?"

"Yes."

Peyton just looked at me then. I grabbed the remote and flipped channels until I found a reality show—stupid drama to make mine seem small. I scribbled the cons side of the list until the pen caught in the middle and ripped the paper, leaving a stripe of ink on my knee.

CHAPTER 12

AARYN

Day 17

Karma was at the game a week later.

She trudged to an open spot on the sidelines, baby carrier on one arm, two bags and a blanket on the other. After a long process of shedding her things, she tightened a gray sweater around her waist and rocked the carrier with one foot. Scanned the field. Danny shocked us both by running up for a kiss right before kickoff. His jersey blocked my view. A white number 30.

She glanced up when the kiss ended and caught me staring.

The ref's whistle shrilled. Time to focus on the team, Danny and his so-called talent. I ordered him to take the field as a starter, ignoring the questioning look from the quarterback. I was in charge. Danny's ego had to be fed. I smacked his back. "Let's go, Danny, you got this. Show the team what you're made of."

He jogged to the line of scrimmage while I folded my arms over my chest.

My plan flopped. First play, he fumbled. Walt lost it for a second and stomped around, hat whipped to the ground. One of the wide receivers saved Danny's ass by scooping up the ball and running it in for a touchdown. A score on the first play! The fans loved it. They were on their feet, cheering, including Karma. A textbook was open on the blanket. I kept Danny in for the rest of the quarter.

At the start of the second, Danny asked for a break and spent ten minutes ordering junk food from the concession stand. He didn't buy anything for Karma.

About five minutes before the end of the half, Nell started wailing. Karma patted her, bounced her, smiling like crazy, talking with really energetic language. Danny joked with his buddy on the sideline. Three little girls surrounded Karma, and though she seemed calm, it was obvious she wished their parents would get them away from her so she could deal with her screaming baby. She stood quickly and glanced at Danny, who was tipping the last of the chips into his mouth.

I meandered over and tapped his shoulder. "If you need to give her a hand, that's totally fine."

"Nah, Nell never stops crying for me," Danny said.

"Yeah, 'cause your *face* scares her," his buddy said. Danny smacked his arm and his friend grinned. They leapt up to spar a few feet behind the bench.

"I need you to take over the next few plays," I said, pointing my clipboard at Walt's chest.

"Ha. What for?"

"There's someone I need to check on."

"Can't you wait until halftime?" His tone was more commanding than questioning.

"This can't wait."

I passed the concession shed with my hands in my pockets. Picnic tables, a cooler—the fans really went all out. I made my way over to the blanket. The three little girls scattered.

"Hey," Karma said with a little laugh, Nell squirming against her chest. "I was hoping she'd make it until halftime."

"Is she okay?"

"Tired. We're always tired, aren't we, sweetie?" She kissed Nell's cheek three times. "I like what you've done with the team. A score on the first drive must be a Lakefield High record."

"Thank God for that receiver."

Her smile faded. "Yeah."

She sat on the blanket and moved her English book out of the way. After a moment of hesitation, I joined her. The blanket was smaller than I'd thought. Soft fleece. The place where we'd accidentally bumped arms seemed heavy with the memory of her touch. I rolled my shoulder around and stared at the field.

"How's Leah doing these days?"

"Oh, her mouth is healed now—not even a scar."

"Does she always speak in a British accent when she's drunk?"

"Accent? Seriously?"

"She 'ad a bit of an accent at the party," I said.

"Wow. I'll have to tease her about that. She's watching Nell after the game so I can go to dance. Trying to stay out of trouble." Karma smoothed the curls that kept blowing over her mouth, one hand holding them back.

"Think that will work?"

"I don't know. I get so mad at her for partying. Ugh, she acts so stupid! But I know exactly how she feels. She just wants to have fun." Karma frowned. "A little fun can change your whole life. I've never regretted Nell, but some days are really hard; today for instance, me taking her here, hoping to get homework done and support Danny, but all she does is cry and—wow, this sounds bad, doesn't it?"

I sat back. "Not at all. I admire you."

Karma snort-laughed. "Me?"

"Yes. You're a strong person. A good mom. I like that about you." For some reason my pulse was racing. Did he ever say anything nice to her?

"Well, that's the end of the half," Karma said. "Look, there's Daddy." She waved her daughter's fist. I forced a smile as Danny jogged toward us.

Good.

Her getting his attention was good.

"All warmed up for the next half?" I asked.

He bobbed his head. "Damn straight. Hey—think you could let me start? You won't be sorry, I swear."

I did *not* roll my eyes. "I definitely think you're ready."

Karma fidgeted, waiting for him to acknowledge she existed. Finally she nudged him. "Kiss?" she said.

After a quick peck on the lips and a pat on the head for Nell, he shot his mouth with water from his sports bottle. "Man, what a game." He dodged imaginary players, sweat running from his hairline. "That first play was pure magic. Did you see how the defense was all focused on *me* so our receiver could sneak in?"

"Aaryn and I were just talking about that," Karma said. "You're still coming to dance tonight, right?"

He guzzled water and bounced from cleat to cleat.

"Danny." She caught him with her hand until he stood still. "That's tonight?"

"We can't put this off any longer." Her voice went quiet. "Juliette's really on my case."

"Do you need me, babe? You know if the guys find out, I'll never hear the end of it."

"Find out about what?" I said.

Danny's hands shot out, palms up. "She wants me to do this dance thing with her."

"You said you wanted to help," Karma said. She smiled, but her lips trembled at the corners. "It's just one piece."

Danny smacked my arm with the back of his hand, like we were friends. "I don't know where she comes up with these crazy-ass ideas. Her little dance hobby makes her a bit . . . woo!" He circled his finger alongside his temple.

Even though her baby had fallen asleep, Karma began swaying with her. She tossed her hair and tried to push by Danny, but he caught her arm.

"Babe, come on. Don't sulk. I'm sorry I can't go, but you have to understand—"

"Fine. Okay." She tugged her arm, but Danny held tight. He squeezed until her sweater came up through the gaps in his fingers. "You're hurting me," she said. Was he? I stepped forward just as he released her.

"Don't mention this dance thing to Ma if she asks. You know how she worries. Take a chill pill."

"I won't." She pressed her cheek against Nell's pajamas.

"What's all involved with the dance?" I asked.

Karma turned with a shrug. She seemed really, really sad.

"Three weeks of rehearsal. Well, it was supposed to be six

weeks." She looked at Danny's chest. "It's for a scholarship I'm trying to get. A big one. The competition is in Milwaukee, so we're going to stay in a hotel overnight. Danny was going to help me perform a pas de deux—a partner dance—because none of the girls at school can do it. They're too small, or injured. Peyton has this ankle problem. Anyway, partnering is one of the requirements."

Maybe I sucked at making him love her, but here was something I could do. "If it will help you guys out, you know, if you need someone, I'll do it," I said. The bleachers were a safe place to stare when I offered. "I took a dance class once."

Danny hooked his thumbs in his gear. Karma's mouth fell open a little. She was still rocking Nell. Did her arm really hurt from him squeezing it?

"All right," she said. A gust of wind blew hair over her face, but she didn't bother to sweep it away. The emptiness in her eyes killed me.

"Cool, man, cool—I guess you *do* owe me your life," Danny said. Adrenaline shot up my spine, surprising me, like I could punch him and not even care.

I did care, of course. He was my only way home.

He pivoted Karma into his arms, baby and all, kissing her hair, her lips. I tried to feel relieved that he was kissing her again but couldn't, probably because the fact that he might not love her was giving me anxiety.

"You're sure this is okay?" she asked.

"I don't care what you do," Danny said.

She smiled as he ran over to join his teammates. "Do you want to meet here after I drop Nell off with Leah?" she asked. "We can ride together."

I stared across the field. Walt was giving me the eye. "Can we leave now?"

Buckling Nell safely into her carrier took five minutes.

When she was in, Karma slid behind the wheel and raked her fingers through her hair from roots to end. The scent of her shampoo, coconut, filled the interior. She was beautiful.

She was.

I noticed and then thought I shouldn't notice, but there:

She sat with her hands full of tangled brown curls, her lips slightly parted. She was beautiful and there was nothing wrong with noticing. She reached up to secure her hair in a bun, but the hair tie shot between my feet.

"Dammit." She leaned forward, her arm pressing against my knee. "Where did it go?" Our eyes met just as she released her hair. It cascaded around her shoulders. "Oh well, I'm sure someone has an extra."

I focused out the window. Lakefield at dusk. We passed empty yards and porches, one kid riding his bike down the sidewalk, no hands. I cracked the window, enjoying the scent of the outdoors, so different from the honey-hint in the air on Mount Olympus. We dropped off Nell with Leah and were on our way.

An old tree by Juliette's road reminded me of home. Someone had placed a plastic face on its trunk, bark-colored eyes, nose, and mouth.

"Look, it's Daphne," I said, pointing to the tree.

"What?"

My smile vanished. "Daphne. The girl who became a tree."

Karma raised one eyebrow. "This I have never heard."

The myths. Stories humans didn't know were real. Fictionalized on purpose, important details left out. But the stories had actually happened. Real gods and goddesses, real lives. I cleared my throat.

"You've never heard the myth of Daphne and Apollo?" I turned in my seat to face her. She shook her head. "Well, Eros—you know, the cupid? He shot Apollo with a golden arrow, causing him to fall madly in love with Daphne."

"And she was a tree, right?"

"She wasn't a tree at first. Once Apollo was shot with the arrow, he chased her. The girl freaked out and begged her father to help her escape. He turned her into a tree."

I didn't tell Karma about the wall that had been built around Daphne, protecting her from prying eyes. Now only the tips of her branches were visible inside the city.

"That's messed up," Karma said.

"Crazy gods," I agreed.

"What happened to Apollo?" She flipped the visor forward to block the setting sun when we started down the road to the studio. "What did he do when she became a tree?"

The inside of my mouth felt hot. "He stayed with her forever. It killed him to see her like that, but he vowed to tend her as his tree and used his powers of eternal youth to make her leaves evergreen. They're known as bay laurel leaves. They never decay."

Pink light from the sunset caught on her face when she tilted it to the left. "It's tragic if you think about it. For someone to believe they're in love with a tree."

I fidgeted. "Yeah."

She scoffed with a rueful half smile. "You'd think, being gods, they could forbid something so stupid. Tree love."

"Yeah." My body felt like stone. "You'd think."

CHAPTER 13

KARMA

The studio seemed alive and smelled earthy from the diffusers Juliette had placed inside the entry. Swishing sounds, dancers' feet hitting the floor, Juliette calling orders—the room was a blur of motion.

"You can just leave your shoes under the bench, and I'll see if Juliette can find some clothes for you to wear."

My aunt sashayed her way over with a cup of tea in her hand. The word *Inspire* labeled the mug. "What's this?" She smiled at Aaryn, freezing the look as she locked eyes with me.

I unzipped my bag. "You remember Aaryn. He's going to help with the competition."

"Oh?" She drank. "Not . . ."

I grabbed my spandex shorts out of my bag and rummaged around for the tank top. "Danny can't come." The words left sadness in my chest—all the movement he'd miss, all the rehearsals we could have had together. Now it was Aaryn who'd be there, Aaryn who'd see me every night and ride in the van and stay up late when it was all over.

"Welcome back," Juliette said. "Maybe it was fate all along, like you knew you belonged here."

Aaryn grinned. "Ha. Maybe."

Juliette sipped her tea and looked over the cup at the girls, who were staring and whispering about Aaryn. Svetlana was fixing her hair. "We better get started," Juliette said. "I'll grab something for you to wear."

"Hey, you two." Peyton walked up, then squeezed my elbow. Her hair was pinned in a tight bun, but waves crinkled along the crown of her head, curls that wouldn't go straight. "Come on, Karma, I'll come with you to change."

The changing stall Peyton crowded me into was dark and smelled like cedar. "What's going on?" she whispered.

"What do you mean?"

"Him. Aaryn. What's he doing here?"

"He's going to do the pas de deux." I used the wall for support and peeled off my jeans, kicking them until they dropped into a stiff heap on the floor. A cricket had snuck into the studio and was creaking nearby.

Peyton helped me unlatch my bra. "I thought Danny was doing the dance."

"He doesn't want to." Why had I worded it like that? Why did it feel like those words belonged on the cons list? I shimmied into my shorts.

"He's not weirded out by some other guy dancing with you?"

"This is what dancers do. I'll dance with tons of guys. It's not like we're going on a romantic date. We're going to rehearse."

"I *know*."

The changing stall curtain scraped open. In unison, we said: "I'm changing!"

"She's changing!"

Peyton jumped in front of me.

"He needs to get in there. You girls can talk later." Juliette was holding a pair of sweatpants. "Don't worry, he can't see."

I snapped my tank top on and meandered into the studio, fixing the edge of my shorts more than once. Aaryn was surrounded, Monique telling him something about her history with ballet. Svetlana stood the closest.

"Are you a really good dancer?" she asked him. She had her ankle pulled up to her head.

"I guess we'll find out."

"I thought you said you'd taken a class," I said. With my heel planted on the floor, I squatted back to stretch.

Aaryn paused. "I've danced."

"You don't know the first thing about dancing, do you?"

"Did Danny?"

Monique and Sofia looked at each other. I stopped stretching. "You'll have to practice a lot."

"I know. I can do this," he said. "I want to do this for you."

He looked so serious, and really out of place surrounded by a bunch of dancers. I kind of felt like a jerk for grilling him. Juliette waved the sweatpants in his direction before I could apologize, and as soon as he turned around, Svetlana pretended to faint.

"Oh my God, Karma, you're so lucky," she said.

"Yeah—you know me, so lucky." I gave a sarcastic half laugh.

"We all know you're going to win yours." Her tone wasn't harsh, but it wasn't friendly, either. I *was* lucky, she meant, and I should be able to admit it.

My stomach felt unsettled. "You guys all have a really good chance at getting the scholarships you applied for. I'll still help you with your allegro steps if you want."

She shrugged. "That's okay. I'd rather watch TV."

Aaryn sauntered out, acting cool, but he kept wiping his hands on his sweatpants.

"Let me think—three weeks," Juliette said. She thought out loud a lot. "I'll have to add another room to the hotel reservation. Shining Waters will cover all your fees."

"Okay," Aaryn said.

Heat rushed to my face. Right. Of course he wouldn't be staying in the same room as me and Juliette, like Danny would have. That's the thing about teen pregnancy—no one in your family tries to pretend you're still a virgin or that you and your boyfriend aren't sexually active. Embarrassing as it was to admit, we *hadn't* been intimate since Nell was born due to me being unbelievably busy all the time—but family and friends just assumed, I guess.

"We'll start every rehearsal with a short class." Juliette killed the music. "Girls, take a break at Kindred for now. I'll be in soon with some interval training."

When the girls left, the room felt really big, just the three of us now.

"Karma, why don't you start?" Juliette said. "Show Aaryn the piece." She stood next to him. "Don't worry, I've choreographed it with a nondancer in mind. Watch this dance—and then we'll discuss more about the pas de deux."

She wanted me to perform for him. Just like that. "Right now?" I said.

"Yes." She pressed play on my performance music.

CHAPTER 14

AARYN

Day 17

I crossed my arms as Karma strolled to the center of the studio. All I had to do was help her secure a scholarship that would fund her lifetime dream.

No wonder Danny had bailed.

Organ music, something really girly, was playing over the loudspeaker. The room seemed huge as Karma sank to the floor with her eyes closed. She sat there. A woman started singing. The first lyrics: *Kiss me hard,* and then the drums picked up.

Karma stood.

A dramatic curl of her entire body.

Her feet followed the beat until she arched, one knee down, toe to the sky, arms in perfect curves. She leapt forward, turning, turning, turning across the floor, her body a blur until it became perfectly still, then blurred some more. Watching her dance was almost like watching . . . a goddess.

Juliette stepped forward. "One, two, three, four." She clapped the beat, her voice strong and commanding.

Karma traced the ground in time to the music, rolled, then jumped up with a series of tight pirouettes. Juliette had a small smile on her face. She knew.

She knew this girl didn't belong in Lakefield. She didn't belong with Danny or in a life she couldn't control. She didn't have a "little dance hobby."

The music cut just in time to hear her gasp for the last move, a deep backbend that finished the song, and with that sound in my ears—her breathing—I felt the trouble I was in.

CHAPTER 15

KARMA

Aaryn's gaze was gentle when we locked eyes, and there was a hint of a smile pulling his mouth, this nervous, kind of shocked smile.

"Wow," he said. "That was really good. Really, really good."

I bowed as a burst of happiness filled me, then hurried to stop the music, which had started over, and got my pointe shoes. "Ready to learn your parts?"

"I have no idea."

Juliette stood before him and held out her arms. "In the beginning you'll stand like this. Karma will dance her parts around you. You'll go"—she moved his arm position twice—"and then she'll stand here." She glanced over her shoulder and waved me into his arms. There was just enough space for me to fit between his hands and chest, like we were at a middle school dance, leaving the exact amount of inches between our bodies. His hands hovered along the sides of my hips.

Juliette tipped me forward, supporting my weight with her hand in the center of my chest. "The pirouette will only work if you lean forward while he holds you steady."

"Hold her steady where, exactly?" Aaryn asked.

Juliette reached around me and took Aaryn's hands. One. Two.

She pressed them over my hips.

"Like this."

His touch was gentle. Juliette pushed his wrists down, her mouth very straight, probably not so sure if this was going to work. His chest grazed my shoulder blades. The next second we were standing arm's distance apart.

"Hold her tight, Aaryn. Do not be afraid to *hold her*. This pirouette is simple compared to the lift you'll practice, and lifts can be dangerous."

In the reflection of the windows, Aaryn squeezed my hips to show that he understood. My breathing was very, very shaky from the last piece.

Juliette walked backward and used a hand-rolling motion. "Karma, try the pirouette and I'll see how your angles are."

I rose onto the shoe boxes, though lifting my arms I accidentally bumped Aaryn's nose.

"Oh my God, no." Juliette shook her head. "Start over."

Could she tell that my arms were trembling?

"Hey," Aaryn said. "We've got this." His mouth nearly touched my skin.

With a sharp inhale, I was up in an attitude en avant with my leg lifted and bent at the knee, as perfect as one of those glass ballerinas on a music box. Ready for the pirouette—the position I'd practiced since I was a little girl. Instead of his gaze,

I met my own in the reflection and saw the fearless dancer I'd become over the years. Shining Waters was always the place I could shed being a mother and a student and a confused girl-friend. I could become the other part of me. I could be flawless.

"Lean her forward, Aaryn," Juliette said. She seemed to be holding her breath. "Remember, you have to hold her. You are in control."

He was strong. The ease he held me with was surprising, like maybe he understood more about dance than I thought, lies and all. He instinctively tilted my torso. I didn't wait for Juliette's cue. He had me, I could feel it, the way his fingertips dented the curve of my hip. My pointed toe sank toward the floor and with strong legs I pushed, hard.

He let go so I could spin, then took me back and held me, keeping us steady and sharp.

"That was good!" Juliette didn't even try to hide her shock. Aaryn laughed a little, his arms falling to his sides.

"Well done," I said, and coaxed his fingertips into mine, enjoying the way his grin faded as I placed his hands over my hips once again. Slowly I turned my back to him.

The reflection, that's where I got his attention. A distant, ghostly image. I stretched my arms up with confidence. The trembling was gone.

"Again," I said.

We did. Two times. Three.

Each pirouette helped our bodies understand each other—the callus on his palm, the slender shape of my hips as I spun. I was breathing heavily, but I didn't feel tired. I wanted more.

I stumbled forward at the sound of rocks spraying in the driveway. A truck had pulled in. Aaryn grabbed me so I wouldn't fall, my back pressing into his chest as he squeezed.

"I think Danny's here," I said, trying to sound cheerful. He'd never come to dance before.

"So he *wants* to do the pas de deux now?" Juliette said.

"I don't think so. I'll talk to him." I untied my pointe shoes and went outside in bare feet.

Danny was leaning against his truck with his arms crossed. "Why are you so sweaty?"

"We were practicing." I ran the back of my hand over my forehead.

"I tried calling like a hundred times."

"Oh. Sorry, I didn't hear my phone." I reached for his hand, melting as he squeezed back. "Is something wrong? Whatever it is, we can talk about it."

He pulled his hand back. "Do you like this Aaryn guy or something?"

"What? No, Danny." The gravel seemed very loud as I switched feet. "No. He's just helping me. You said you were okay with this."

Was he glaring at me? It was hard to tell what his look meant as he peered from beneath his baseball cap.

"Why'd you tell Ma you're going to file for child support?"

"I never said that."

"Yeah, okay, well, that's not what Ma said. She told me all about your little phone call last week. How many times have I told you—keep Ma out of our business?

"Next thing I know, she's blowing up at me about how she can't afford to pay child support for Nell, since she'd be responsible, me being underage, and going ballistic about me getting papers signed and figuring out my life and—Christ."

I pushed my bare feet against the driveway. "That's not what we talked about, I swear. I only mentioned . . ." I swallowed to erase the ache in my throat. "I only said it would be nice if you helped. Got a job. You're going to need money for college, aren't you? Your mom told me about the scholarship." I wavered, shivering from the air that seemed to be seeping into me. "Why didn't you tell me it was only a thousand dollars? The way you said it . . ."

Danny's eyes were shadowed beneath. "Is that all you care about? Money?"

"No!"

"Yeah, okay."

"I'm still happy for your scholarship, I am. Any money is better than none. But . . . it's not easy to pay all the bills on my own. That's why child support is there for single parents, to help out. With you moving to Louisiana, and me to Mississippi—"

He banged the metal. "So you *are* going to file papers, then?"

"No. I just mentioned needing help, especially with us graduating this spring and . . ." I watched for his reaction to what I'd said, my little clues. *With us moving. With us graduating.*

"So this is more like a threat than an actual decision?"

My throat closed up. No, I wouldn't cry. "I'd never threaten you. Your mom misunderstood what I was saying. Can we just forget this? Nothing's going to change."

"It better not."

I snuggled against him and tried not to notice that he winced. The feel of him, safe. My everything. My head fell against his shoulder, needing him, the warmth of him holding us together.

"I want this plan to work," I murmured. But my chest felt vacant, as if I could feel nothing in that moment, not even hope. "We can still see each other every weekend."

"Okay," he said.

My hand pressed against the side of his stomach. "Are you sure that's what you want? Sometimes I can't tell, and it scares me." I lifted my face. "Do you want us to go with you?"

He was standing very still, and his breathing had deepened. "Sure," he said.

He didn't mean to hurt me. But as he wrenched away, a quick push to untangle my grip from his waist, my forehead caught the side of his truck mirror. I gasped. I bit my lip to keep from crying.

You'll see him every weekend.

A trickle of blood ran down my temple.

To be honest, I'm not sure he saw what happened. I'm not sure he knew I was hurt. I pivoted and began to walk toward the studio, taking small, quiet breaths to keep from sobbing. I wanted to remember the moment for the good parts, not the bad.

"Get back here!" Danny said, apparently changing his mind about leaving. "Don't walk away from me." He grabbed my arm, and when I turned, he was forming a fist.

The studio door flew open. It happened so fast, Aaryn sinking his hand around Danny's neck and shoving him against the truck, a scuffle of feet as they charged for each other.

"Don't you dare push her like that. What's your problem?"

I held my breath as a sob escaped my lips. Aaryn had been watching us, and Juliette probably saw it all, too. It couldn't have looked good, the way Danny twisted away from me, the way I lost my balance.

"You want a piece of me?" Danny spat. His voice weakened as Aaryn's grip tightened.

"You hurt her."

"Aaryn, stop that! He didn't know." I wiped the blood away, but it wouldn't stop. I held my face. "He didn't push me on purpose."

Aaryn was breathing hard and staring Danny down. I'd never seen his arms ripple like that. When Danny lunged at him, I knew my words had come too late.

"Stop it! Both of you, stop it!"

Fists landed, thudding into the dark. I couldn't stand it. They rolled. Aaryn was fast, calculating, almost as if he'd been trained to fight. A few seconds later he held Danny down. "I don't want to hit you again, but I will," he said.

"Fuck you," Danny managed.

I pushed Aaryn with all my might. "Please." He didn't move. "I said it was an accident."

Juliette ran out. "What's going on here? Danny, Aaryn, get up, both of you. Cool it. God, Karma, what happened to you?"

"I hit my head by mistake."

Aaryn watched me. For a moment there was only us, him searching for me to tell her the truth, me wanting to cry. He shoved Danny just as I felt I might throw up.

"If you ever hurt her again . . ." Aaryn leapt up and stalked toward the back of the studio, ripping weeds with his hands as he passed. Danny jumped to his feet with clenched fists, shoving me out of the way, but I immediately blocked his path. "Don't," I said.

"Don't follow him," Juliette said. "Enough."

His lip was swelling up. "It's not worth it," I said.

Panting, he took another step forward and yelled, "Coward!"

"Sort out your problems somewhere else," Juliette said. "This is a sanctuary for us, not a fighting ring."

I pressed my hand against his chest. "Please, if you love me, you have to leave now. I don't want anyone to get hurt." I swiped again at the blood trickling down my forehead.

Danny left without saying goodbye.

I listened to the sound of his truck fade into the night until there was only me and my aunt and the country, a mosquito humming around my head, the wild of night all around. My throat felt like it had collapsed, it ached, but I stood in silence until I couldn't hear Danny's truck.

"What did he do?" My aunt's voice was scaring me. I shook my head and broke into a run toward the back. Aaryn stood in the darkness near the pond, facing the studio, arms crossed. When he saw me, he tugged me into the light.

"You're still bleeding."

His T-shirt came over his head. One hand held my shoulder. The other pressed the cloth against my wound. "You should report him, Karma."

I couldn't enjoy the sight of his naked chest, though part of me wanted to. The sculpted muscles, perfectly shadowed, perfectly smooth. His flat, touchable stomach. Boyfriend or not, I wasn't dead. I shrugged his hand from my arm. "How many times do I have to say it was an accident?"

"I saw what happened. We both know what he did."

"Was Juliette watching?"

"No."

The sick feeling came back, sour and intense. I couldn't think straight. "He came to tell me we're going south. All of us. In the fall." The lie came out so easily.

Aaryn stared. "Awesome."

I wasn't going to break down in front of him. "Sometimes you have to make sacrifices for love."

Aaryn smoothed the clean side of my forehead, and at the feel of his fingertips, my eyes closed gently. "Maybe your feelings for Danny aren't what you think. Love shouldn't hurt."

The rhythm of the crickets, the urge to go to him, to lean into that chest. I opened my eyes. "What makes you the expert on love?"

Aaryn shrugged. "I know your boyfriend shouldn't push you."

"I told you, he didn't!"

"I know what I saw."

I swallowed and lifted my chin. I wouldn't give him the benefit of arguing. "I'm going to get my things," I said. "I can't rehearse anymore." I wiped my eyes and walked away with my hand clutching his shirt. Things would be different in the South. Less stressful. More focused on us. Yes, the move would be a fresh start, one we desperately needed.

I wouldn't feel so empty there.

CHAPTER 16

KARMA

"What the hell happened to your face?" Leah asked.

"Nothing," I snapped. I hurled my things at the corner and tiptoed into the kitchen, every muscle in my body sore from dance. Home. Finally. That silent car ride with Aaryn had been as stressful as waiting for competition results.

The freezer opened with a gentle *whoosh*. Bags of vegetables, leftover casserole, pizza, ice cream. Normal things. Comforting, homelike things. I lifted an ice pack, wrapped it in a flowered towel and eased it against my forehead. Ouch.

"Nothing, my ass." My sister blocked my path and pulled away my hand for a better look. "Did Danny do this?"

I rolled my eyes and tried to push past her. "Don't be dumb. I fell at rehearsal."

"You're lying." She clamped both hands on her hips. "You always look out the window when you lie."

I faced her as my spine stiffened. "Danny didn't push me. Is that better?"

"I never said anything about him pushing you!"

I was already halfway down the hall and barely heard her words. She chased me.

"Don't shut me out." Her hand slammed against the bedroom door. I gaped at her, my head freezing, heart pounding. The scared look on her face, almost terror . . . I didn't know what to do. I couldn't tell her the truth. I didn't even know what the truth was anymore. She crowded me inside and closed the door with a click. My little sister, so grown up. Dark eye makeup. Hair straightened into thick, even lines.

"You don't have to lie," she said.

Nell stirred in her crib, and even though she didn't fuss I went to her. Reached for her. Feeling her against me, warm and perfect, the emptiness didn't matter as much. I buried my face against her neck, soaking her in. Leah sat on my bed.

"It was an accident," I whispered. I steadied my breath and eased Nell onto the comforter next to my sister. I loved watching her sleep. Leah leaned in, too. We sat like that for a while, Nell between us.

"You know how I feel about him," Leah said at last. I stroked Nell's hand and sighed deeply. I did know. She'd made that perfectly clear for more than a year. "Why do you put up with it? You deserve so much better."

I rolled my eyes and crawled toward the pillow, lifting the ice pack. "I'm tired," I murmured.

Leah flounced toward the headboard and grabbed the other pillow, bed creaking.

"Don't wake her up!"

My sister winced as Nell squirmed. The last thing I wanted to deal with was an overtired, screaming baby. Thankfully, she didn't open her eyes. I shot Leah a look. *Think a little.*

But inside I was glad she was there. No words needed, and nothing complicated. Just us sisters.

"Do you think I'll ever get married?" Leah whispered.

I snorted softly. My sister was a weirdo. "Probably, many, many years from now." I turned, my hair catching on the cotton pillowcase. "Where'd that idea come from?"

My sister slid her hands under her cheek and stared at me across the bed. "I was just thinking about it today. . . . Will you be my maid of honor?"

"You're engaged?" Nell twisted and I grimaced. Quieter, I said, "You can't get married until you're eighteen."

"I *know* that." She pinched the base of her nose. "I mean when I find the right guy. God, relax." Her eyes met mine. "I was just thinking that I want you beside me in the church."

I reached over to smooth a rebellious cowlick above her forehead. "Of course. I'd be honored." I gave her a serious look. "But you better raise your standards a little. Benjamin doesn't seem to have much going for him."

"I'm going to marry Aaryn," Leah said, rolling onto her back.

I shook my head, a smile pulling my mouth. "Quit it. He's too old for you."

"Age won't mean anything once I turn eighteen. That's the kind of guy I want to marry—someone hot and sweet." She turned fast. "Do you think he's rich?"

"How would I know?" I resituated the ice pack and exhaled shakily. "We don't get time to talk about his personal life."

Leah bolted upright. "Time to talk? What do you mean, time to talk?" She bounced a little closer. "You didn't tell me you talked."

"He's partnering me," I said, like she should have known.

Her wide eyes amused me. "Danny was busy, so Aaryn volunteered to help in his place."

Leah gaped. "Wow. That's nice of him." She shrunk back and squinted a little, pursing her mouth, lost in her own thoughts. The ice cracked as it began to thaw.

"It's just one piece," I said. "Once you're eighteen he's all yours." Then I turned over, not liking the expression on her face. That smug look, like she thought she'd uncovered a secret about me.

"You can have him," Leah whispered. She sounded so earnest. She nestled Nell between us and carefully stretched out. "I was just kidding about before."

"Thanks but no thanks." I stared at the wall as my heartbeat quickened; my gaze following the edge of the only print I owned of *The Ballerina Project,* my favorite photo series of dancers posed all over New York City and beyond—feet arched on Broadway, arms outstretched with Long Island City in the background.

Through the window I found the moon and let the thin crescent of light slip out of focus.

CHAPTER 17

AARYN

Day 18

Karma sped the entire way to rehearsal, her music playing un-usually loud. "I just love this weather," she said as we pulled into the parking lot. "This has got to be one of the nicest falls we've ever had in Lakefield."

"Yeah," I said.

She hurried into the studio while I followed with careful steps, the screen door nearly smacking the side of my nose.

"Whoops!" she said.

And in that moment when she turned, I got a good look at the cut, a dark line along her eyebrow with ragged edges. Danny was such a creep.

"So, back to the grind," she said, meaning dance. "I'll go change."

"Okay."

She gave a dramatic sigh when she scraped the changing stall curtain in place, though she definitely didn't make eye contact. I sat on the bench. Studied my knuckles, which were sore from yesterday.

"You're feeling good enough for rehearsal, right?" she asked. Her voice was muffled. My hands held the edge of the seat.

"I felt fine until I got a good look at what he did to your face."

The silence that followed grew into an enormous sound, throbbing in my ears. Karma emerged with a frown so deep, I sort of felt like an asshole. "Sorry," I mumbled, but I wasn't that sorry. She couldn't pretend last night hadn't happened. I didn't care how great the weather was—she couldn't make up some story about what Danny had done to her, because I knew what I'd seen and—

To my right, the door slammed. "Well," Juliette said. "You're back. We need to get to work." Her flip-flops made a slapping sound as she paraded past us with a stern expression. "Danny's not going to ram over here tonight, right? I can't have problems like that at my school."

"He's at Dmitri's," Karma said.

"Good."

Karma's mood seemed to be darkening by the second. I hung back as she walked to the center of the room, hoping she'd sense that I didn't want to hurt her, only help her.

The music blasted and Juliette didn't waste time, clapping beats and shouting at us, but Karma lost her footing once, then twice. Touching her felt wrong when she was mad at me. I moved my arms the way Juliette had shown me and held Karma for the pirouette, but it was hard to focus on her, especially when she might meet my eyes.

"This isn't working," Juliette said. "Let's take ten." She faced Karma with one eyebrow perked, mouth in a sour circle, like she expected her niece to leave all her emotion at the door and focus. Like it should be simple. Juliette left. Instead of shrinking when Karma tried to walk by me, I moved into her way.

"What?" Karma asked. She rolled her eyes.

"Something's bothering you. Are you pissed at what I said?"

"I just wish everyone would leave me alone."

"You know we can't. I'm worried about you. A lot's happened."

Karma stretched her neck and eased onto the floor in a split. She picked at an imperfection in the wood with her fingertip. "Danny told me about the school meeting."

"Yeah." I cleared my throat and shrugged a couple of times to help shake off the reality of the past twenty-four hours. "Walt fired me."

Losing my job for punching Danny was bad, but not as bad as things were between us now. If we did cross paths again, which was pretty unlikely given that I wasn't his coach, he'd probably want to beat me up. Plan B? I had nothing. What I did have was a growing realization that my mission on Earth was totally screwed.

"He shouldn't have said anything," Karma said. "I mean, the fight was a total misunderstanding. I tried to tell him that, but he didn't care."

"Well, too late now."

Big shock here: getting Danny to propose by punching his face hadn't worked.

"I don't like fighting," Karma said. "It's unattractive."

"I know, and I'm sorry. I don't know what came over me—when I saw you were hurt I just snapped, out of instinct."

"He wanted me to kick you out of the competition."

"He did?" And, wow. The thing that scared me the most? For a second, all I cared about was not being able to spend time with her. Something was really wrong with me, especially since I only had seventy-two days left on Earth.

She brushed her hair forward until it covered half the mark. "I told him it was too late. You're the only one who knows the piece."

"I don't want to come between you and your boyfriend," I said. Being reasonable. Karma was nodding really fast.

"Oh, I know. I agree—yes. We'd have to stop if he asked me to."

Well. He *had* asked her to kick me out. "I guess he probably hates me, huh?"

"Yeah." Her voice was soft. Almost afraid. "But he won't come back here again. He promised."

"I'm sure he'd like to land a few punches on me."

"He's not going to do anything."

Neither of us was too sure.

"Well, whatever. I'm not going to worry about it," I said. I tugged her up, liking the fact that she bumped against my chest. Danny couldn't stop us. He'd tried and she'd said no. "The most important thing we can do now is focus on your scholarship. We can do better." I held my hands out. "We can win this."

A little smile lifted her mouth. "Oh?"

"Yes. I'll work harder. You deserve to win."

You deserve a life.

"Hmm." Karma sauntered over to the sound system and pressed play, then tiptoed in front of me fast. Her waist fit against my hand in a perfect curve. "Ready?" I felt the vibration of her voice. She twisted and I held her, softened my grip, and pulled her back with my hands. Strong girl. Beautiful girl. Dancing with me. Maybe Danny hated me, and maybe he'd never be nice to her, but this was nice. She spun again, talking through the steps to stay in sync.

There had to be a way to fix things with Danny. I'd think of a plan. Soon. We stumbled a little but found our places again without mentioning it. We went on like that for many moments. She fell back and caught herself on my arm.

"I've got you," I said. She shook her head, smiling, and tested her balance as she rose. It was a while before we realized Juliette was watching.

"Oh, hey," Karma said, and for some reason she took two steps away from me.

"That was good." Juliette sipped her tea. "You two look great out there. Really great."

"I've got a ways to go," I said, and chuckled, though it didn't change the electric mood in the air. Why did it feel like we'd been busted? Karma practiced her way to the big windows and acted very interested in whatever she'd found outside.

"It's such a nice night," she said. Then the room got so quiet it seemed to roar.

"I'm heading out," Juliette announced. She tipped her cup against her mouth. "You two work as long as you like."

"Where are you going?" Karma asked. Her eyes were round when she turned.

"Just out. The other girls went to a movie. They'll be back before nine."

"Oh."

"We can work on the lift tomorrow. You don't need any-thing from me, right?"

"I guess not."

Juliette looked at me, then left, the door closing softly be-hind her. The sound of her car tires crackling against the gravel gave me a chill.

"I guess we better get back to work," Karma said.

"Yeah." Were my hands okay? I shook them out, but my heartbeat only got more ridiculous. Okay. Enough. I had to focus. Make a new plan and get Danny to marry her. Get back to Mount Olympus.

My hands slid onto her waist.

An hour passed. Karma danced hard all the way through and grabbed us a couple of waters when she noticed the sweat on my face.

"I think that's enough for tonight," she said. She held up her phone. "Danny texted. He's picking up Nell for a sleepover. Giving me a break. Isn't that nice?"

"Is he okay watching her?" I asked.

"He's her dad. And Judy will be there to help. She's raised four boys." She was still breathing heavily from practice.

"Oh."

"Can you kill the lights?" she asked. "I want to show you something."

I turned the light switch off.

"Isn't that cool?" she asked.

The pond behind the studio danced with light. The strands were strung around the dock pillars, creating an outline. I tried to ignore the fact that I wanted her in my arms again.

"Sometimes I dance out there," she said. "It was my favorite place to go when I was little. Just me and the water and the dock under my feet."

"Sounds like a great childhood."

"It was, for the most part. I just wish my mom hadn't struggled so much, with Dad being gone. Raising two girls by herself wasn't easy." I felt her face turn to me. "I've never really known my father."

"Oh. Wow. I'm sorry."

"It's not that big a deal. I mean, it is, obviously. I probably have deep-seated daddy problems, but between my mom and Juliette and Nell keeping me busy, I've never had much time to think about the bad stuff." She seemed to be convincing herself more than me. Her hands clapped together. "I should teach you how to swim."

I guess Danny had filled her in on my inability to even tread water. "Sure." My adrenaline shot up. "I'm game."

"Come on, Jones. The next lesson begins."

Before I could do the foolish thing I was thinking and pull her close, she headed out of the studio and led us to the pond.

The school grounds felt really wild in the dark, like we were going on an adventure. Crickets sang from the woods.

"What do I need to know?" I asked.

She was wearing her dance clothes—spandex—and as always, they looked good. They'd probably feel amazing in the water, all slippery and smooth. No.

There would be none of that.

I took off my shirt and kind of hoped she'd notice, which officially made me a freak who didn't listen to common sense. Getting into the water with her seemed more and more like a terrible idea. She was staring at my bare chest. Decision made.

Water sloshed around me as I walked in, my toes sinking into the sediment.

"Look at that," she said. There was a line of silver in the water from the moon, but I didn't spend much time admiring it. The water came up to her chest, curving there.

"I love it here," she said. "This is my place." She grazed the water with her hands.

"Are you cold?" I asked. I didn't think, I just moved right behind her until her shoulder blades pressed against my chest. "Maybe we should practice in the water."

"What?" she said. I heard the smile in her tone.

"Let's try it." And I placed my hands on her hips, noting that the spandex did feel as good in the water as I'd thought, and a way crazier idea of tracing her neck with my mouth practically choked me with desire. Just as my cheek brushed the side of her hair, she dove under and swam away.

"Hey!" I said. The feel of her wake rippled against me.

She bobbed up, grinned, and made a bad attempt to splash me.

"There are only two things you have to remember," she said. Her voice sounded small. "The first is not to panic. The second is to move your arms and legs like you're dancing. That way you won't sink."

"But I'm not good at dancing!"

"You know how to dance." She demonstrated the swim stroke above the surface. "Go a little deeper and try it."

The water came up to my neck. She was out there in the reflection of the lights, the dark woods—there was no denying the moment between us.

Go to her.

I did, though not as gracefully as I'd hoped, my eyes just above water. She smiled as I drew closer and rolled away from me in the water, twisting, and I began to paddle, splashing to keep up with her.

"You're swimming!"

The water didn't feel cold at all.

"What do you think?" she asked.

"Awesome." But water got in my mouth. I imagined I looked pretty stupid half thrashing around. So much for my cool act.

"What are you going to do if I drown?" I asked, coughing a little, not great at avoiding the drink.

"Drag you to shore and give you mouth-to-mouth?"

I held my breath and faced her, my head going under.

"Not falling for it," she said.

I thought I had the whole swimming thing figured out, but when I finally burst through the surface I was coughing, and Karma had to pull me along and smack my back a bunch of times.

"Are you okay?" she asked. "You shouldn't mess around like that."

"Well, you dragged me to shore," I said. "Next part?" I let out a whoop as she smashed water toward my face. I started to swim strong, back toward the center of the pond.

"You're bad," she called. Then she ran in and began to power swim toward me. I met her, churning water as fast as I could. We were laughing and out of breath. Water beaded on her face and gathered in her eyelashes, both our heads bobbing. When I ducked for shore, she joined me, and once we could touch, I took her hand.

"Spin for me," I said, like I wasn't just trying to hold her hand.

She twisted, slippery thing that she was, and looked really, really happy. "The water feels good after dance, doesn't it?"

"Yes." There was a lot that felt good about our swim lesson, and a lot that felt scary, but I wasn't about to elaborate. The water swirled as she turned again, using my hand for support.

"There's something forbidden about this, like we're Johnny and Baby," she said, but her tone was light. "Like we shouldn't be spending time together. I don't know." She seemed fine with hanging on to my hand.

"Wait—who and Baby? Your baby?"

"Baby from *Dirty Dancing*," she said. "You know, the old movie with Patrick Swayze?"

"Never heard of it."

She splashed my face, which kind of annoyed me until I opened my waterlogged eyes to find her shaking her head.

"You're kidding me. That's tragic. Come inside. Juliette has the collector's edition."

The chill space, as Karma called it, had one huge couch, lots of pillows, and soft lighting. I tried not to think it was romantic, because Karma wasn't like that with other guys, and I wasn't thinking romantically about her. So, yeah, where was I? Right— the gigantic, too spacious couch.

I sat on one side and Karma sat on the other. She'd dragged her backpack along and had a sheet of homework ready to start. The distance between us, every damn inch, felt like a wall of bricks pressing against me. It was just blank space—fabric and cushions and air—but I felt it. The divide came with instructions:

Do not move.

Do not pass this place.

Don't act like an idiot.

Something I wasn't exactly known for.

"Peyton and I love this movie," Karma said. She tossed me a blanket, which felt good since I was wearing a pair of thin athletic shorts Karma had found in Juliette's closet (I didn't ask) and had left my T-shirt at the pond. "You're in for a treat. This movie is the best." She lit up when she was that happy.

She handed me a bowl of popcorn and a huge jar of ice water with lemon, then settled in across the Great Divide with the same things. The screen glowed. At least I could hear her munching popcorn over the sound of my heartbeat, which was stupid, the way it hammered like something was going to happen between us.

Nothing was going to happen. Maybe I just had water in my ears.

"Is this a super-girly movie?" I asked, pretending to be annoyed.

"Shhh."

I aimed and tossed a piece of popcorn at her head. Direct hit. She brushed it out of her hair.

"Can you act civilized and watch the movie, or is that too much to ask? I have homework."

"Maybe."

"Danny says it's a boring chick flick, but I call it a classic." Her pencil scratched the paper for a few seconds.

I decided to love the movie no matter what. Homework had

her full attention for five minutes. I lobbed another piece, pretending to be really into the movie as it scuttled across her assignment.

"You!" she said. The paper fell. She whipped a piece back, which I popped into my mouth, eyebrows up. She laughed, and we took turns aiming for each other's mouths, but then she got a little weird and fidgeted until she was straight-faced and bent over her homework.

The movie was all right.

Awkward might be a better way to describe it. Dirty dancing—no lie, that's really what it was about. The one character, Baby, stumbled on a secret party during a family vacation where everyone was, I am not making this up, "dirty dancing," and then stuff happened, and she was dirty dancing with Johnny, her major crush. The whole movie was nothing but a tease. All I could think about was dancing like that with Karma, which felt wrong and awesome and started to make me crazy.

"I know this dance by heart," Karma said, pointing with her pencil to the scene with Baby and Johnny. "Peyton and I mess around with it in the studio—I play Johnny and she plays Baby. Ha!"

I shoved a handful of popcorn into my mouth. Bad, bad, bad, bad—

"Hey!" I rubbed the spot on my forehead where a kernel hit.

"Can you talk?" she said.

"About what?"

"Just conversation, I don't know. I said, 'I play Johnny and she plays Baby,' and you just sat there like you didn't care."

Girls could be so clueless. "I care." I turned to face her. "But I'm sitting here thinking there's not much to say to that except maybe . . . what else happens when you practice dirty dancing? And I'm not sure either of us wants to go there."

"Great, now you're making it sound dirty."

"Well, that *is* in the name of the movie."

"You don't have to be gross."

"Me?" I sat up with a smile, gaping. "You're the one who brought it up. I can't help it if my mind wanders."

She gave a short cough, stood, and strode toward me until her silhouette blocked the TV. "Okay, Mr. Wandering, now you're twisting what I said. I never meant for you to *go there* with any of this." She stopped before she got too close. I did something very stupid.

I stood.

The Great Divide was gone. Well. She was the one who'd crossed it.

"Hmm, are you going to teach me a lesson?" I asked. I held up my hands in mock defense. "Don't hurt me." Her mouth wobbled into a smile.

"Ugh!"

I caught her hands in mine as she lunged. She was smiling and her eyes were glittering and I was in serious, serious trouble. She struggled playfully and it was all too much. I was done for. Logic, bye-bye. I didn't care about Blackout or Danny or Mount Olympus or the girly movie in the background because all I wanted to do was kiss her and feel her hands on me and never stop.

She turned her face away when I tried. I played it off like I'd tripped—cursed once and grabbed the toe that I'd apparently "stubbed on the floor." You know how those floors get in the way. She said something like, "You're missing the best part," and then returned to the opposite end of the Great Divide, where we proceeded to finish the movie in a very proper fashion, light flashing across her face when the scenes changed, her knees drawn up to her chin, her thumb brushing along her bottom lip.

CHAPTER 18

KARMA

"Roses?" The next day, Mom slid two grocery bags onto the counter and worked at smoothing the top of her hair. "Are those from Danny?"

I rubbed one of the petals between my fingers as I finished arranging them in the vase. "Aren't they perfect?"

"What's the occasion?"

"Oh nothing. Just because." I started to tell her about the double date he'd planned for us, which was happening in about ten minutes, but she gasped and gripped my arms.

"What is that?" She held my chin and tipped my head toward the light. "What happened?"

"Mom, let go." For someone who always wanted me to take responsibility for my life, she sure knew how to smother me. "I'm fine. I fell at dance." I twisted away and pulled the vase into the crook of my elbow. "I'm going out. I'll be home by curfew, okay?"

"What about Nell?"

"Leah is babysitting so we can have a date night."

Mom's brows furrowed. "You're not going to rehearsal? Juliette said you got a new guy to help with the scholarship."

"Aaryn. He's from Florida." The vase was ice-cold. "I have to get ready."

"Sweetie, let's talk."

Great. I switched the vase to my other arm, the blooms brushing my shirt. Mom pushed her hand along the table, then tapped her knuckles twice. "Is something going on?" Her face twitched. "You've been acting funny lately."

I let out a big sigh. "No, Mom. I'm just busy."

"I'm not doing this again." Her voice was low. "I'm not going to sit here while my daughter spirals out of control like last year."

"Mom, trust me, it's not like last year. It's one date night."

"Does this have something to do with the other boy?"

"No, Mom, definitely not. Aaryn's just a friend." *A friend who tried to kiss me.*

Ten minutes later I was out the door.

"Finally." I grinned at Peyton, who had her hand extended through the open truck door. Nick hopped out to let me in. The weather was muggy, but my dress was short and my hair was twisted in a knot. I climbed in next to Danny and kissed his cheek.

"Prodigy." He smelled like mint gum.

"How are you?" Peyton asked. "Aw, that cut looks painful. I can't believe you fell."

I flipped the visor and pulled the hair forward over the mark. I'd parted my curls to the other side to hide it better. "I'm *fine*. Can we talk about something else, please? Mom and Leah are driving me insane." I shook my head and adjusted the AC.

Danny revved the gas and sped more than necessary across the bridge.

"Easy there, killer," Nick said. He had to curve his head forward to fit in the cab. He slid his arm around Peyton when he realized Danny had no intention of driving his truck like anything but a race car. Miraculously we made it to the Sports Cage in one piece.

The Sports Cage was part bowling alley, part restaurant and bar. Plenty of deals were made in the maze of dimly lit hallways and rooms—some kids sold weed, or found a girl to ask out, and the girls were known to commiserate in the bathrooms where all the best rumors were shared. A pop song blared from the speakers.

"Thanks for planning this," I said, settling into the booth.

Nick held Peyton's hand as she slid into the seat and she beamed. They were cute together. Danny set his phone on the table and checked his messages until the waitress handed each of us a menu.

I tried to ignore the fact that Peyton and Nick were soft-talking to one another about the options while Danny waved his menu like a worm, the vinyl crackling a little.

"What are you getting?" I asked.

"Double cheeseburger."

"I think I'll have the grilled chicken salad."

He rolled his eyes. "You and your salads."

I picked at the menu's edge just as I caught the end of Nick and Peyton's conversation. "... no chicken dinner on our wedding day."

She laughed and shoved him a little. He pretended to fall out of his side of the booth.

"*Nick,*" she whispered. "We're in public."

He righted himself and sipped his water with one pinky out. He loved riling her, and as always his goal for the evening seemed to be making her smile.

"Did you just say wedding day?" I said. Dishes clattered in the kitchen and it was hot in there, too hot, like the windows hadn't been opened in thirty years.

Peyton sucked a small ice cube and waved her hand. "Yeah. Nick's just being weird."

"You guys are getting married?"

"No, shhh, don't say that too loud in here." She leaned forward. "Too many spies."

Nick stuck out his bottom lip. "I asked her to marry me, and she turned me down flat."

"I did not." Peyton poked him. "Don't tell people that, jeez."

"Well, you did!"

"I said we're too young." She tossed her hair and held it back with one hand, looking at him with a really soft expression. "Ask me again in two years when I'm an RN. Maybe we can get married before I go for my bachelor's degree."

Nick bowed his head. "I got a ring and everything." He slammed his fist over his heart. "Nurse! I think my heart is dying. Nurse."

"*Nick.*" If she smiled any wider, her face might get stuck.

I stirred my water, dunking the lemon below the ice. "Why wait if you know you're meant to be together?"

The table shook as Danny jiggled his knee. He stretched his

neck to one side and the other before proceeding to crack each one of his knuckles. A couple of girls from school walked by and waved at him.

"I want to do that dance thing with you," Danny blurted out. The rest of us fell silent. "So. Yeah." He made a spitting sound through his teeth. "You can let what's-his-face know that he doesn't have to come to practice anymore."

The air felt suffocating as I inhaled. "Really?" A girl walking by accidentally bumped Nick with her purse. "You'll do it now?"

"Yup."

My finger traced a ring of water on the table. "We have to work a lot. Every night."

"Okay." He sat back, one arm draped over the side of the booth. "Whatever you need, babe."

I cleared my throat, but it felt like there was something caught in the back. "Can you come tomorrow after school?"

"I got football practice."

"Oh, right, I forgot. How about after?"

Danny made a face, then began tipping his head back and forth like a pendulum. "That might work."

My heart was racing as I smoothed the napkin over my thighs. "If you're going to commit to this, we really have to practice."

He took my hand and squeezed, then lifted it to his mouth. "I'll be there."

We dropped Peyton off first, then Nick. The truck idled in the driveway as we watched him saunter in.

"Let's get out of here," Danny said. The feel of his lips

brushing my ear helped me relax. The engine roared. I scooted over and kissed him, my stomach fluttering as he pushed back, that old fire we both knew so well. It had been too long since we'd had sex.

"You taste good," he said, and massaged my thigh.

"I've missed you," I said. He was changing. The flowers, dinner, now the scholarship. He was going to be better. He was going to live up to all of the pros on my list.

He inched down my thigh and drove off. I knew where he was taking me.

He turned down a gravel road toward our hideout. We hadn't been there in a long time, too long, and sparks spread through my body from head to toe.

He pressed my hand against him and groaned when I melted toward his chest. I unbuttoned his pants.

The abandoned hunting shack was at the end of a rutted trail, our lover's escape. We'd made out—and then some—surrounded by those same trees, those broken windows. Danny settled against the door with his eyes closed, petting my hair. A few seconds later I kissed him with wet lips.

"I want you," I whispered.

He nudged me downward. "You know what I like."

His stomach was soft and smooth beneath my cheek. I loved us like that, him alert and wanting and mine. After a few minutes, I edged alongside him.

"Do you have a condom?"

He cupped my breasts, massaging me, his eyes ravenous, familiar. "I . . . don't think so."

"Oh. Well, then . . . we can't." I sighed and sat back. "I missed a pill last week."

"It'll be fine, babe." He tugged me close, but I couldn't kiss him the way I wanted to. I couldn't let things get too far.

"Stop it. I'm not going to be stupid."

He groaned. The truck was really quiet as we sat there in the dark, each of us staring out the window.

"Sorry," I added.

He zipped up, whipped his gaze over his shoulder, and backed out of the woods.

CHAPTER 19

AARYN

Day 19

Idiot.

She'd known I was going to kiss her. And she'd made the line I'd almost crossed perfectly clear.

Case in point, she cancelled our next rehearsal, though I told myself I had no idea why. I also didn't know what she planned to do instead and hadn't been obsessing about it all day. In fact, I hadn't wondered once what she was doing since I hung up the phone, because I didn't have time. There was too much to do in less than seventy-two days. Save Phoebe and myself from Blackout, for instance.

And Phoebe. The guilt I felt for liking Karma—stupid!— while Phoebe waited for me to fix things. While *we* had a thing. What if Phoebe could see me from up there or some god was watching me, filling her in?

The piece of paper on the coffee table was blank. I wrote *Plan* across the top.

Pressed my fist against my skull.

Impulsively I scratched a series of stars on the page, connecting them with fast lines. Maybe Diorthosis could align the stars for me, and Danny and Karma would live happily ever after. I wrote *Aaryn Jones's request* and drew an arrow to my constellation.

With a groan, I stalked over to the kitchen window and opened it. No breeze. I pushed them all wide, every window, and stood in front of the screen in my bedroom with both hands gripping the sill.

Then I felt him.

I turned. A guy stood behind me in black clothing, his dark hair a point in the center. He looked half ghost, half human, but he was neither.

"Tek," I said. The ring of black around his eyes made his gaze that much sharper.

"Hey, Aaryn." He nudged his chin toward me. "Nice place." The floor creaked as he took a few steps around the room.

"You're . . . here."

"Yep."

"How can I see you if I'm human?" I asked.

"Must be a special human."

"Ha."

He didn't laugh back.

I crossed my arms over my chest and faced him, feeling cornered next to the window. "I know about the audit."

He shrugged. "That wasn't my fault, man. You can blame Zeus for finding out what you did." He squinted his neon blue eyes. "Wouldn't recommend that, though."

He observed me as if I were an alien. "You don't belong here," he said. "Come home with me."

"I can't leave until I fix things." My knees felt wobbly as I strode across the room and I sat on the couch. Did he know I'd tried to kiss her?

"I want us to work together," Tek said. "Things are different now, you know. Your father and I have joined forces. Phoebe and Chaz? Everyone's on board."

"Is Phoebe okay?"

"Yes." His form wavered. "She comes to High Tower with Chaz. They're good at what they do."

"What do you mean? What's High Tower?"

"My headquarters. Eros and I have big things planned."

"Dad's working with you?" Tek nodded. Maybe Dad was the one observing the mess I'd made on Earth. Maybe he'd sent Tek himself. "He knows you're here?"

"He knows the plan."

"I have plenty of time to finish my mission." I grabbed the paper with the stars that lay on the table and folded it in half. "Things are going well. I'm confident that I'll be able to succeed in time."

Tek studied me. "You'll never go to Blackout. I promise. There will always be a place for you on Olympus. Forget about this mission, this game, and think about the future. You could lead us. See for yourself." He stretched his hands into two L-shaped corners, and instantly a screen appeared before us. Images of a skyscraper began to flash, mirrors covering the building. Beyond them a labyrinth had been created, with thick white dividers. Gods and goddesses reclined in oversized chairs, their gazes fixed upon screens suspended in air. A glass-topped bar advertised free champagne.

"Phoebe . . . ," I said, and sank against the cushions.

She was there, laughing at something Chaz had said. Life had gone on at home, making it clear: I had to stay on Earth. Someone actually needed me here. Karma's life wasn't a game to me.

"I know a secret," Tek said suddenly.

"Yeah, you and everyone else at home."

He squinted. "You know the story about how your father left Psyche, didn't want to be tied down, all that?"

I stared.

"Well," Tek continued. "As you know, your mom has been living in the country outside Mount Olympus since the split. What you *don't* know is that your dad forced her to hide there. With Aleth."

"Forced her? And who's Aleth?"

"Her lover. Now you know. Your mom left Eros for Aleth."

I frowned. "That's believable."

"Aren't you curious?" He stretched his hands, the video appearing for a second, leaving an orb of light in my eyesight. "Aren't you wondering how on *earth* your own mother broke the arrow's spell?"

A chill spread over my skin. He was radiating light, a smirk on his face. "There's no way she broke the spell," I said.

"Unless the lead arrows still exist."

"Dad ordered Hephaestus to destroy that formula hundreds of years ago. They're all gone."

"Okay. If you say so. I just thought, given the fact that you're still enjoying the luxuries of your little mission, you might like to know."

"Why would Dad shoot my mother with a lead arrow? That makes no sense."

"Maybe she used one on herself."

"No. She wouldn't."

"Maybe love isn't as sacred as you've been led to believe." His presence had the faint odor of something burning, the scent thick in my lungs. "Forget the mission. You could leave tonight."

"Yeah, good idea." Fear was a machine that hummed in my ears. "You're just full of good ideas and stories, aren't you?" The thought of failing Karma paralyzed me. "What have I been thinking all this time? I'll just leave."

Tek reached into his pocket and held out a square item the size of a postage stamp. Light shimmered through it in waves. "Take it."

"Not sure what that is, but no thanks."

"It's a chip. Dissolves instantly under your tongue." He pressed it into my hand, where it felt twice as heavy as it looked. "Use it and you'll be a god again. All you have to do is pop it in."

"I think you better go." I stood and took a step sideways. The corners of the chip dug into my palm when I squeezed. But then I hesitated. I was used to gods and goddesses trying to get close to me for the sake of their own power, and now the benefit could be mutual. "Are you sure the chip will work?" I asked slowly.

"Yes. As soon as you're home I'll know, and I'll help you with everything."

"Then why don't you give Phoebe a chip? Save her from Blackout."

Tek grinned. "Done. Phoebe's already safe. Things don't always have to be so complicated."

I stared at Tek, a guy no older than me, who had somehow worked his way into all the gods' secrets. He stood there, waiting, confidence licking through his skin and clothing like voltage.

Hope unwound inside me.

"Bring me a lead arrow."

CHAPTER 20

KARMA

I couldn't hide the storm from my face when I threw my dance bag into the cubby. Three days later and once again I'd come to rehearsal alone.

"Uh-oh." Peyton strode toward the entry and peered over my shoulder as I rummaged around for my dance clothes. "Did Danny bail again? Oh jeez, he did, didn't he?" She hugged me.

"He's got a lot of homework," I said, like I was some kind of robot reading Danny's stupid text out loud.

Peyton scrunched her mouth. "We all have homework." She sat before me in lotus pose as I changed. "But we're here."

"I know." My clothes slammed into my bag. "I know, and I don't know what I should do. I'm so mad, and I don't even know how to tell him I'm mad. I'm . . . hopeless."

"Aw, don't say that. Just tell him he's out. Aaryn would probably do it again. Tell Danny to go frick himself." She pointed to my knee.

"How? He's on some kind of power trip about Aaryn after

the fight and everything. How do I tell him this isn't okay without him thinking I just want to spend more time with Aaryn or something stupid like that?"

"He should have come to rehearsal if he cared so much."

The spandex snapped into place. "I'm calling Aaryn. You're right. This scholarship means everything to me."

More than Danny? No . . . or maybe it did, just in a different way. A way he certainly didn't understand. Peyton hugged me again. "He'll get over it."

"Come on, girls," Juliette called. "Time to get to work." She beckoned us forward.

"I'll be right back." I grabbed my phone and scraped the changing stall curtain closed. I punched the buttons to get rid of Danny's text, which was still blazing when the screen came on.

Aaryn answered after the second ring.

"Of course I'll still help," he said, and it was the best thing and the worst thing, and all I could do was sit on the plank seat and say thanks.

"Hey," Aaryn said.

"Yeah?"

"Things are going to get better, okay?"

"What do you mean?"

"Just trust me—everything will get better."

I scooted into the corner of the changing stall. It was dark in there, with a thin line of light along the bottom of the curtain. "You're acting weird," I said.

"I know."

I drove to Dmitri's after rehearsal so Danny and I could talk, because of course he was there, "doing homework." My muscles ached, my eyes, my voice, at the thought of arguing with him again.

"So." I killed the car engine once Danny slid into the passenger seat. No point in wasting gas. He smelled faintly of cigarettes. "Um. Look. I need a *reliable* dance partner." Little chills coursed through me, like I couldn't believe I was being honest about how I felt. Then, through the window of the shack, I swear I saw Jen peek out. "Is . . ." I leaned toward the steering wheel. "Wait, is Jen here?"

"Uh, not that I know of."

I kept my gaze glued to the square of light. Dmitri's piece-of-crap couch was empty in the background. After many awkward seconds of silence, and a war going on in my head over what to do, I unbuckled.

"Okay. It's fine if he does the dance," Danny said. His voice seemed too loud. "I'm sorry, I should have been there for you. I understand that you need someone who has more time for something like that."

He took my hand and drew me close for a kiss, a long kiss, but all I could think about was how I needed to go inside and prove that I wasn't going crazy. Jen had been there. My heart pounded in my ears as he pulled me farther and farther from the door. I tore my mouth away. "I saw Jen. She's here, isn't she?"

"Babe. What?" He had a shocked expression, his eyes darting all round. "It's just us guys in there. Bros before hoes, you know how we roll."

"Bros before hoes?" My eyebrows couldn't go down any farther.

Then my phone started buzzing. Great. Mom was calling,

probably because she was having a hard time putting Nell down. Nell always slept better after she knew I was home.

"Why don't we plan a date for the weekend?" Danny said. "That would be fun, right?" My phone stopped, then started again.

"Yes, okay. I could use a break."

"Love ya, babe." He jumped up, slammed the door, and took his time wandering back to the shack, little glances my way. Almost as if he was guarding something.

CHAPTER 21

KARMA

Two weeks later I loaded enough suitcases and baby gear into Juliette's rented van to survive an apocalypse.

"I wish I could be there," Mom said. The sun hadn't even risen yet. Four in the morning and we were all up except Nell, who slept in her car seat.

"I know," I said. "But Grandma needs you." My grandmother, who lived two hours north, had taken a fall earlier that week, which meant Mom was the only daughter available to stay with her for a couple days after she was discharged. We hugged. She felt soft in her oversized sweatshirt. She felt like home.

"I'll send pictures," I said.

"I'm so proud of you." Mom's voice trembled in my ear. "You're a good girl, Karma."

"Mom. Stop it."

"I'm serious! I know I don't tell you enough."

I lifted Nell's carrier. "Make Leah help you."

"She said she's really busy this weekend," Mom said.

"I know what she said." I also knew a lot about what girls said when they were planning to party without their parent knowing. I trudged into the back of the van and Nell woke up immediately.

"Coffee," Peyton yawned, one row up.

"Here, have a drink of mine." I handed her my to-go mug and stuck my head out the van door. "Bye, Mom. I'm serious about making Leah go with you."

"Good luck." She was teary-eyed, and I had to admit my throat felt small. I ducked in to avoid a cry-fest. Really, though. It was a big moment for our family. We had survived a lot of hard times, maybe not gracefully, but we had. I had. This time Nell would be at my competition, both my joy and my burden. I sighed and wiggled a pacifier against her mouth.

Juliette headed for Aaryn's apartment, our final stop before we got on the road. The van was a utility type, boxy with a door that didn't close itself.

"I want Aaryn to sit by me," Svetlana whispered, turning so just we girls would hear. I glanced at the empty spot to my right. Oh well.

His hair was still wet from a shower when the van door whirred open.

"Good morning," he said. He sounded way too cheerful.

"There's room up front," Svetlana said, patting the seat next to her enthusiastically.

"I'm good." He edged in next to me, brushing against my arm. "Are you ready for this?"

"I should be asking you the same question."

He offered me a granola bar.

"Thanks." I tore the wrapper and crumbs spilled onto my lap. I shook the carrier gently to soothe Nell as I tried a bite.

"Are you nervous?" I asked. A piece of oatmeal stuck to my lip.

"Yeah." He chomped his bar in half. "Aren't you?"

"I'm always nervous until I feel the stage." We were at the stop sign where Main Street met the highway. "Once I'm up there, I'm ready."

"I wish I had your confidence."

"You'll do great."

He sat back and our arms touched more, and after we pulled onto the highway everyone in the van fell asleep.

We made it to Milwaukee before nine-thirty a.m. Since it was too early to check in to our hotel, we unloaded our gear at the front of the Milwaukee Dance Studio. The street was alive with movement. Dancers, parents, and coaches swarmed toward the double doors.

"I have to change Nell's diaper," I said. The city was white noise: people walking by on their cell phones, motors whirring in buildings and cars. There were no birds in sight. I always thought opportunity lived in those sounds, so much more than the country sounds of Lakefield. "I'll be back."

Everyone around me carried dance gear, while I threaded my way to the restroom with my baby in my arms, diaper bag on my shoulder. Nell smelled like poop.

Then I saw a sign outside two enormous doors that read *Leona Barrett Scholarship* and hesitated for a better look. My gaze panned the room the way a movie camera circles a truly amazing place. The stage was dotted with spotlights. Rows and rows of black folding chairs had been set up in front. My audience.

"Look at that," I said, edging Nell close. "Mommy's going to perform up there. Isn't it beautiful?"

She seemed to understand, and stared in awe like me. Several dancers milled around the room, some of them practicing, others with headphones on. Nell gurgled to whoever cared to listen.

"Oh yeah?" I said. She yawn-cooed a reply. Okay, diaper time.

A line of girls waited outside the bathroom, but lucky for us there was no line for the baby-changing station. I switched Nell's diaper as fast as I could, dabbing a little cream on her butt, and met up with the others in the hall.

"I brought the rest of your stuff," Aaryn said, patting the rolling luggage beside him.

"Oh wow. Thanks." I knelt down and rummaged through the diaper bag for Nell's bottle. She was working up to her spastic wail. "Shhh, shhh, shhh, almost ready."

"I can take her," Aaryn said. "No puking," he instructed as she squirmed in his arms.

"Oh my gosh, your baby is so cute!"

A girl who looked no older than thirteen crowded Aaryn, three others following her.

"She's not mine, she's—"

"What's her name?" crooned one of the girl's friends.

My face felt red-hot. I edged into the group to take her back, but Aaryn shrugged and waved me away.

"Nell," he said. He grinned and positioned Nell so the girls could coo at her, which helped. She stopped crying for a full twenty seconds. Once Nell started wailing again, the girls left.

I found an outlet to plug in the bottle warmer and sat against the wall, bouncing Nell while she wailed and spit out the pacifier. A few people looked at me funny when they walked by. The worst was this girl so beautiful she didn't even seem real, who was followed by two older women and a kid carrying a sign. Her fan club, I guess. She made a face, like me sitting next to a baby bottle with my baby was the weirdest sight she'd ever encountered. The bottle warmer dinged.

"Okay, girls." Juliette looked fresh for having gotten up at four a.m. Nell sucked the bottle and drank in long, sleepy gulps. "Let's figure out your schedules."

Svetlana, Sofia, and Monique were dancing for a few of the other scholarships being sponsored, and Peyton was along for moral support, since her ankles still weren't the greatest. Also, she'd agreed to babysit.

"See anyone you know?" Aaryn asked. The hum of everyone talking, Nell drinking, a few girls looking my way curiously—I felt dazed.

"No," I said. "No one looks familiar." I wasn't a ballerina anymore. Not like past competitions. I snuggled Nell against my chest and began burping her, which she did loudly. With a smile I kissed her cheek.

"Ready for me to take over?" Peyton had a cup of coffee in her hand and seemed a lot more awake. Her hair was full along the crown, a thin headband tucked around it. Wrapped in hemp and beaded. "I think I'm going to check in at the hotel so Nell doesn't have to spend all day with her meal plugged into the hallway."

"We're used to improvising," I said. The dancers were really flooding in now. "Are you sad you're not competing?"

"Not really." She set down her coffee and wiggled her hands around Nell. "I love competing, but not when I hurt."

"I'm going to grab a water," Aaryn said. "You guys want anything?"

"I'll take one," I said. Peyton shook her head. He was a magnet for female attention as he retreated down the hall.

"So," Peyton said. "Aaryn's quite the guy, huh?"

I dug my schedule out of my purse and began checking it over for the hundredth time. "He's very nice." I had one hour. First up, a group class, then a modern solo, then pointe work, and finally a pas de deux—in my case, the piece with Aaryn—to show off my partnering experience.

"You guys seem to have a good connection."

"We do." I met her gaze. "There's nothing going on between us, if that's what you're implying."

"Did I?"

"Don't be cute." I reached out and drew Nell's shirt over her belly. "I know you."

Peyton eased Nell against her other shoulder. "I'm just saying—he's really great."

"I know."

She made a pouty face. "Sometimes I wish you had a nicer boyfriend, that's all. And he's so nice!"

"I don't want to talk about this."

"Okay."

All those people in the hallway, the sound of chaos, mostly, everyone preparing for one of the biggest moments of their lives—it felt a little claustrophobic. I folded the paper and shoved it deep into my purse.

"Your water, my lady," Aaryn said.

"My lady?" Peyton said. She nudged me. She was totally smitten. I took a step away from her. Aaryn tipped his bottle against mine. "Cheers. To a great performance." He drank, sighed with satisfaction, and glanced around. He was in a really good mood. "Should I be doing something right now? Warming up?"

Okay—yeah. He was nice. And good-looking. And thoughtful. But it wasn't like that between us.

He held out his hand. "Come on. Let's find a place to work in *private*."

I could feel my stupid face burning when we touched. I did a little spin for show, I don't even know why, and tripped because some clueless group of dancers bumped into us. Aaryn made a big scene of catching me. He scooped me up and said something cheesy like "At least wait until we're alone."

"Put me down," I said. My heart was pounding because I knew Peyton was taking it all in, like she knew more about the kind of boyfriend I should have than me.

"I know just where to take you," Aaryn said. "And yes, you're welcome. I've done my research." He motioned for me to follow, really enthusiastic. I went to him.

The supply room was empty except for supplies—toilet paper, soap, and cleaning products on rows of metal shelving. We rehearsed a little, a good warm-up before the group class. The steel door was shut tight and blocked the noise in the hall.

"There's some really tough competition here," I said. "Did you see that girl practicing in the hall?" I spun, his hands on my waist, the pirouette flawless.

"I've never seen anyone dance the way you do," he said. "Seriously. You have a gift."

"Thanks, but now I'm even more nervous."

"I can give you a back massage if you want. Here, lie down."

"What? Um, no, that's okay."

He winked, because he'd been joking, and heat radiated through me. Juliette had always said there was a little bit of truth behind every joke. I stepped away from him, smiling, the edges of my mouth twitching. "Do you have a girlfriend?" It would be so much easier if he did. Being friends with him would be so much safer. "There has to be some lovesick girl wishing you'd come back to Florida, right?"

He shook his head. "Hate to break the news to you, but I'm a total loser no one likes."

"When was your last relationship?"

"About a month ago. This goddess—I mean, girl—I knew, she was really fun and pretty and all, but things didn't work out. She wasn't that nice to me. I guess we just stopped liking each other."

"Have you ever been in love?"

"I don't know." He reached over and moved a strand of hair from my forehead. Dust particles floated, tiny flecks of diamond. "What's love feel like, anyway?"

"Hmmm." I stared at my bare feet, ugly from all those years of dancing. "I guess, I don't know, like magic. Like a flash. All of a sudden I just knew Danny was the one." The burn in my stomach spread into my chest.

"And you never question things? Your feelings for him?"

"I wouldn't say that." The scary part was that I wanted Aaryn to know that *yes,* I did wonder sometimes if Danny and I would last, even when it felt painful, literally painful, to imagine a life without him.

Admitting it, though? Dangerous. Almost like I had led him into my pond of poison that could potentially ruin everything.

Maybe, and this was probably dumb, but maybe he was the antidote. He held out his hand and I took it. He was warm and strong as he drew me against him, his face close, too close, everything too hot. The doorknob turned.

"You can't be in here." A man wearing a janitor's uniform swung the door wide and stood back for us to leave.

CHAPTER 22

AARYN

Day 39

She was the best. No doubt in my mind. I stood in awe as Karma moved across the stage for her pointe solo, the music crisp from the speakers.

I stole a quick glance at the judges. One judge had dropped her pen and leaned back in her seat, not even trying to conceal the fact that she was enthralled by Karma's talent. I felt so proud. I felt like nothing in a room where she was everything. My hands actually stung from clapping when she bowed.

"You can continue with your pas de deux," announced a judge wearing horn-rimmed glasses, who looked as old as Zeus. Karma nodded from the stage to invite me up. Okay. I could do this.

I climbed the stairs slowly, going over a mental checklist of what I'd learned so I wouldn't screw up. The spotlight half blinded me. Karma gracefully led me to the center of the stage.

"Ready?" she whispered. She angled my arms for the piece. I swallowed and tried to gaze in the direction of the judges. Were spotlights always this extreme? I focused on her hair instead, noticing that a curl had slipped from her bun. It glistened. I wanted to brush it back, pull her close, tell her how amazing she'd been.

The light blurred and my breath caught in my throat as she began to dance around me, then lifted into position. My hands following her slender hips as she rose. She was tense; the pirouette was coming. The easy part. We'd practiced so many times.

When she moved, my grip fumbled. My fingertips slipped down the bone of her hip as I tried to take hold again, hold of anything—the indent of her torso, her tights. She crumpled before me, it seemed, in slow motion. My frantic lunge to grab her was too late. I landed with two hands over her body.

"Ow." She grabbed her ankle and stared at me, inches from my face, her mouth contorted. One of the judges gasped, and from the corner of the stage I saw Juliette's hand fly up to her mouth.

"Please," Karma said, voice shaking. She pushed my chest and used my wrist to pull herself up, trying to conceal a limp. "With your permission, we'd like to keep going."

"You're hurt," I said, but she turned her back to me.

"Hold me for the lift. We can do this." She rose on her good ankle. The last move of our piece happened so fast, her body as precise as steel against my palms, almost like she didn't need me. She lowered to the ground and bowed. At last one of the judges found her voice.

"That was . . ." Shuffling of paper. "Thank you, uh . . ." Whispering. "Karma Clark. Thank you. That was very brave."

Karma's face flashed in the spotlight, a small smile. I tried to help her leave the stage, but she wouldn't take my arm.

"We have to get that ankle on ice," Juliette said, but Karma didn't stop. Her limp was getting worse. When we exited the auditorium, I nudged her, sliding her arm over my shoulder.

"I'm carrying you."

"Put me down, I'm fine. I'll be fine, I swear."

I gathered her into my arms the way you hold something very fragile, crooking my elbow beneath her knees. She weighed practically nothing.

"Thank you, Aaryn," Juliette announced sternly, giving Karma the eye.

A couple of girls began whispering when we passed them, and in the background the next competitor's music was playing.

"I'm not mad at you," Karma said. Her voice was muffled as she spoke against my chest.

"You nailed your pointe solo," Juliette said. "I'm not going to sugarcoat the fact that Aaryn fell on top of you onstage—but maybe that won't matter."

"They won't dock her for my mistake, will they? They must take into account that I'm not the one applying for the scholarship, right?"

Juliette's mouth pressed together. "Let's get back to the hotel."

Karma felt frozen in my arms, like everything that had just happened was reaching into her, the way water turns to ice. The three of us strode forward with our heads high, though there was no way either of them felt confident. At the double doors, Juliette stood back, allowing Karma and me to move into the narrow entry, which was one of the few quiet areas in the whole place—dancers on one side of the glass, the city on the other.

"You can put me down now," Karma said. I brought her outside and pulled her close.

"No."

The sound of traffic helped create space from the competition, almost like it was a thing we could literally leave behind us. But the truth was, none of us could.

"I'm sorry," I said. "I really screwed up. I don't know what happened." Her head rubbed against me, her bun coming more undone. My T-shirt felt damp.

She was crying.

Sorry wasn't enough for what I'd done to her life. A taxi hurtled past, blaring its horn. I tried not to shudder, but I knew. The lead arrow was Karma's chance for a happy ending. My throat tightened, but I couldn't break down, not here. Not when she needed me to be strong.

For me there was only goodbye.

"I'm taking Nell for a walk in the lobby," Karma said. Her ankle had been iced, then wrapped. Just a minor sprain, according to the nurse practitioner the hotel had called. Karma held Nell's face to her neck, but she bucked and cried. Karma looked like she wanted to join her.

"I'll come, too," I said.

Peyton and Monique exchanged a look. I stood from the hotel chair in the corner of Juliette's suite, the one that had seemed like a good place to hide. The girls had all acted like everything was fine when we got to the hotel, chattering a lot, making small talk. Still. The reality of what I'd done onstage lurked in the room, like me in that chair.

Juliette was in the bathroom with a curling iron in one hand, surrounded by the scent of really strong perfume. "Don't forget, we're leaving in thirty minutes."

"I know. I think a walk will calm her down."

Karma had the stroller handle in one hand, a diaper bag hooked over her shoulder, and a squirming baby against her chest. Her hair had loosened, and her eyes were smudged from crying earlier.

My stomach flipped.

"Do you want *me* to help?" Peyton asked, some silent best friend exchange going on between them.

Karma shook her head. "You deserve a break. You're the best for watching her today."

Peyton kissed Nell's bright red cheek as I coaxed Karma into handing me the diaper bag. "I've got a key," I said.

The hallway felt small as we wound our way to the elevator. Nell stopped crying, which surprisingly only sharpened the awkward mood. After a few seconds of hearing nothing but the sound of our footsteps on carpet, I chuckled.

"You were right," I said. Nell focused on me with wide eyes, drawn by my voice. "She just needed a walk."

"Mm-hmm."

I swallowed and stood with my arm against the elevator door so Karma could pass, then took my place on the opposite side of the car as the display inched down floor by floor. The elevator chimed.

"After you," I said.

Karma fit Nell into the stroller, adjusted the straps, and tucked a blanket over her.

I shoved the diaper bag into the storage pocket. "I'll push."

"I can do it."

"I know you can. Let me help you." I eased the stroller back and forth. "There's no point in pretending you're not mad."

"I'm not mad." She frowned. "I just wanted everything to be perfect."

"Let me make it up to you." I glanced at the hotel exit, which was covered in vintage scrollwork, everything all fancy. "Let's go on an adventure."

Karma smiled the first real smile I'd seen in hours. "An adventure? No, we can't. Where?"

"I want to treat you—you and Nell. Let's get out there and see what we find."

"We can't! The girls are waiting, remember? We're all going to dinner."

"I want to do something nice for you. Just us."

Karma looked at me like I'd read her mind. "I'm so tired of pretending everything's great. I'm dreading that dinner."

"Send them a text. Tell them we're running away but will be back in a couple of hours."

After a second of hesitation, Karma reached for her phone.

The city at night was noisy with traffic, couples going to dinner, groups of girls darting across the street to beat the crosswalk. Somewhere in the distance a band was playing. Nell had zonked out, which was adorable, her fist curled alongside her mouth.

"Sometimes I wish someone would cover me up with a blanket and push me around," Karma said.

"Sign me up."

She smiled as we walked along. "I love the city."

"Me too."

"Have you ever been to New York?"

"No. Never," I said.

"You *have* to go there sometime. It's my favorite place in the whole world. Well, so far. I have a lot I want to see."

"Like what?"

"Ireland. London. There are probably ten places on my list."

"Your list?"

Karma nudged my arm and pointed to Chéri Café. "My bucket list. Look, they have outdoor seating."

"What's a bucket list?"

We stopped in front of the tall windows with white lettering arced in the center. "You know, a list of things I want to do before I die. You've never heard of a bucket list?"

"No." The fact that I wouldn't be mortal much longer seemed like an unnecessary detail. "Table for two?" I asked the waiter. Glanced at Nell. "And a stroller?"

We were the only couple at the café with a baby. The dining area outside was really romantic, with candles on every table and tall outdoor heaters running for warmth. There was a guy playing acoustic guitar in the corner.

"This is perfect, thank you," Karma told the waiter, who held the chair for her. He handed us our menus and we sat down, scanning our options.

"I should have a bucket list," I said. "I want to experience life to the fullest."

While I still can.

I tried not to let the sad feeling creep up. Too late. Tek could come back anytime. I'd break her enchantment, insert the chip, done. I'd be gone.

I drank my glass of ice water fast, spilling a little down my shirt. Karma rummaged for something in the diaper bag, grimacing as Nell began to fuss. She spent the next three minutes rocking the stroller until she fell asleep.

"Okay," she said, but not too loud, a pen in her hand. "Let's do this." She flattened a napkin. "Your bucket list. You tell me what to write down and I'll make it official." Her face looked amazing by candlelight.

"Okay." I paused. "I don't know."

"Just think of something easy, like, hmmm—take shots of tequila until you puke."

"Wow."

"Already checked off?"

"I don't drink tequila."

She bit the end of the pen. "Rumple Minze, then?"

"Sometimes, I swear, you speak a different language than me."

"*Sí, señor.*"

"Are you ready to order?" The waiter had returned. He flipped up his pad.

"Oh, sorry, we haven't looked at the menu yet," Karma said.

He seemed used to this. "Take your time."

We began to scan the selections, the menu blocking her face. "What's fried fromages?" I said, holding my finger to the spot.

"Oh, that's just a fancy word for cheese."

"Fried cheese?"

"Cheese curds."

"What?"

The menu lowered four inches. "You've never had cheese curds?"

"No."

She dropped the menu and wrote *eat cheese curds* on the napkin. She held it up. "You can cross something off tonight!"

"Okay." The list felt a little silly—but a little awesome, too. "I want to try red wine."

"Gross." She watched me, then shrugged and added a second bullet point.

"I just want to try it." Would it taste different from the wine on Olympus? The sharp, warming drink was a tradition after a day on Earth as a cupid. Being human now, it felt like something I had to compare.

"Well, you're on your own with that one." She nodded to the stroller.

Wine was the first thing I requested when the waiter returned. He smiled at Nell, then me, and walked off with our order. Fried fromages, calamari, which was something from Karma's bucket list, and pesto fries.

She squeezed my arm. "I can't believe he didn't card you!"

"Card me?"

"You know, make sure you're twenty-one. I guess he thinks you're old."

"What's so great about being twenty-one?"

Her eyebrow went up. "It's the legal drinking age?"

"Oh." I shrugged and turned my attention to the list. "What are some things we could do around Lakefield for my bucket list? Will you go to some places with me?"

Karma took a long sip of water. "I don't know."

"More adventures?"

"Danny wouldn't like it." She motioned her hand between us. "You and me, spending time together?"

"I get it."

"I can't do that to him."

"Maybe he doesn't have to know."

"I'm not going to lie to him. I hate liars."

Guilt worked into my stomach, and not just because of how loyal she was to him. She hated liars yet was surrounded by them.

After a few seconds she leaned toward me. "Well, like what kind of things?"

I grinned. "How about—I want to cook a nice dinner for us. Fried fromages or something. Something fancy."

"There's nothing fancy about cheese curds."

"Well, we'll look up some recipes, then. Nell can come, too."

Karma smiled and wrote down the idea. "Okay."

My brain was really working now, taking things too far, things she'd never agree to, like *kiss under the stars* and *spend a whole night holding each other.* I cleared my throat. "I want to go camping. In a tent."

The pen dropped. "I can't stay overnight in a tent with you," she said. "That's crossing the friendship line. We have to agree not to plan things that are crossing the line."

"A bonfire?"

"Fine."

The ink made it official.

"A party at the studio."

"Hmmm?"

"I want to have a party with everyone—Juliette, the other students, my landlord; Danny can come if he wants—everyone."

The waiter returned with my wine and Karma's latte. We thanked him. From the look on Karma's face, she really liked the party idea.

"A celebration," she said.

"Yeah." *A goodbye.*

I inhaled so deep, I felt my lungs would burst. Ugh. The thought of going home was different than I'd expected, but there was no point in being sad. I had to go home, and she had to move on with her life. She'd spent more than a year loving Danny—a year chasing him—and the idea of finally giving her life back felt amazing. I tried my wine. Closed my eyes.

"You like it?" she asked.

I nodded. The tingle inside my mouth spread all the way to my stomach. "Cheers."

We clinked, her coffee mug, my wineglass, and shared a second taste.

"Wait, so you've never been to a bonfire or a party before?" she asked.

I shook my head. "No bonfire. I've been to parties before, though. Just not with you." I smiled.

"You've had a weird life."

I finished the wine, feeling too warm. "I might have to move soon."

Her cup stopped at her chin. A woman at the table next to us laughed loudly, but Karma kept her eyes on me. "What do you mean?" Her lips parted. "Why would you do that? You just got here."

My pulse jumped. "Well, I don't have a job now," I said. She folded her hands and leaned her mouth against them. "So my dad asked me to move back to Florida. Work with him. We've, uh, been talking about it."

Karma traced the handle on her cup over and over. Our food arrived, which gave us something to do besides sulk.

I popped a cheese curd into my mouth. "Wow."

"Wisconsin's famous for them," Karma said. Her tone was flat.

"Are you okay?"

"I guess."

"I think we've got a good list there." Maybe mentioning the party would put her in a better mood.

"No, I guess—just no, I'm not okay. I can't believe you're moving. I know there aren't many jobs in Lakefield, but there must be something, somewhere. What kind of career do you want, anyway?"

"Karma." I stopped chewing, the wine suggesting I say things that I knew I shouldn't. Instead of telling her we could never be together, I placed my hand over hers. Her eyes darted to meet mine. Soft knuckles and wrist. A shiver went through me. She didn't pull away. "I have to go. You're with Danny. I don't have a future in Lakefield."

The musician picked at the strings of his guitar. After thinking about what I'd said, Karma turned her hand over and squeezed. "I'll really miss you." She said this with a short nod, blinking fast, and took her hand back. She turned to the music.

A plan I could partly blame on that glass of wine was starting to come together, a really, really far-fetched idea. Blackout lasted three months. Failed gods were sent there as humans with no memory of their former lives. No one really knew how it worked, but I did know the humans were rehabilitated—given new identities, given a trade, and prepared for release into society.

If I waited until the last day of my mission to shoot Karma with the lead arrow—day ninety—and failed my mission before I could use Tek's chip . . .

"What if I come back to Lakefield three months after I move?" I blurted out. "Would you still be my friend?"

Karma raised one eyebrow. "Should I, uh, add that to your bucket list?"

"Karma, I'm serious."

"Serious about what? Moving or still being my friend or—"

"If I move away for a while, I, uh, might not remember you. At least not as well as I do now." More like not at all.

"Nice."

"So you wouldn't talk to me?"

She sighed and shook her head. "You know that's stupid to say."

"I could get a tattoo that says *Lakefield, Wisconsin.* You know, to make it official. Make sure I come back."

"Okay, if you think that's a good idea, go ahead. Maybe you should add *That one girl Karma* to your tat. Or *No regrets.*"

"I'm serious. The tattoo would work."

"I think you better lay off the wine."

Nell started fussing, which was probably a good thing, since I needed time to think things through. Karma kissed Nell all over when she picked her up, and the two of them looked really cute sitting there, Nell with her mom's eyes, both of them a little distraught.

The tattoo might work—a permanent reminder that I had to go there after Blackout, one the gods couldn't change. The lead arrow would work, definitely, no doubt in my mind that she'd leave Danny right away once she wasn't under the arrow's spell. And then she'd have room for me.

If I stayed . . .

We could be together. Her spell would be broken, and she'd

remember these moments. She'd remember: *I'll really miss you.* I wouldn't need my memory to realize she was amazing.

I sat back. I felt weirdly excited, and it wasn't because of the wine. I had a choice. My destiny was not as preplanned as I'd always allowed myself to believe. Choice was power.

I wanted to stay, wanted her, and for the first time since I'd landed I knew there was a chance.

CHAPTER 23

KARMA

That night Peyton and I were up late. The hotel room was dark except for a gap where the curtain didn't fully close, and through that space the city was out there, the streetlights and traffic, no stars visible in the sky.

"I can't believe it's all over," I said. Juliette was on her side in the bed across from us, snoring. Nell was in a playpen next to me. The other girls were in the adjoining room and they were probably up, too, wired from everything that had happened. Aaryn was down the hall. Room 223. I placed my hand under my cheek.

"It was an amazing day," Peyton whispered.

The room felt hot. I flipped the sheet off my side and rolled onto my back. Darkness, gray foreign darkness in a room that smelled like food and dust and too many people.

Peyton sat up on her elbow. "Tell me more about your adventure."

Somewhere in the distance a siren wailed, and little kids

were running up and down the hall, their feet pounding. The hotel room was so different from what we were used to. It felt like we were in a place where anything could happen.

I told her everything—the part about Aaryn moving, the bucket list, him coming back in three months. I rolled over to face my friend. "He said he's getting a tattoo that says *Lakefield, Wisconsin.*"

"That's weird," Peyton said, leaning close. "Why bother moving?"

"I know."

She smoothed the blanket beneath her arms, then started picking at her nails. "Did you talk to Danny?"

I covered myself and sank down a few inches. "I texted him."

"Oh." Like she knew he hadn't replied.

"What was your favorite part of the trip?" Aaryn asked. We were on our way home, all of us a little sad to go, and all of us stuck in some morning-after daze. The girls offered an obligatory glance over their shoulders at him. Aaryn held up his hand. "Mine was when Karma danced her solo." He smiled at me, to his left. "Actually the whole trip was my favorite part."

My face was on fire. I pulled my knees up to my chin, comfy and content in yoga pants and one of Danny's old sweatshirts.

"Well." Svetlana hooked her arm over the seat. "My favorite was meeting Harry. He's such a good dancer. You guys should have seen him."

Monique blew a laugh through her mouth.

"What? He's named after the *prince.*"

"I didn't say anything about that," Monique said. Svetlana rolled her eyes and settled against the window with her phone, presumably so she and Harry could send love notes. We were all overtired and all on the brink of misinterpreting things. Juliette merged onto the freeway.

Peyton leaned over to our side and smoothed Nell's forehead, which caused her eyelids to flutter. "My favorite part was when you got back to the hotel and took Nell for a walk. You know I love her, but wow. She's a lot of work."

I chuckled, holding my hair out of my face. "Really?"

The van slowed to a stop as traffic jammed. "My favorite part," Juliette called, eyeing us in the rearview mirror, "will be when I get this van back to the dead roads of Lakefield."

"That's the worst part," I said.

"You really hate the country that much?" Aaryn said.

"Yes."

"Do you think you'd feel different if you grew up in, say, New York?"

"Not a chance."

"Wow." He held the word, like he was teasing me at the same time.

"I think I'm going to win," Sofia said. "I had a good feeling about how things went."

"You were awesome," Juliette said. "All of you."

My stomach dropped, which made me feel terrible, even though I smiled at Sofia and told her, "That's really good." With a sigh I scooted closer to Nell's car seat and spent a long time watching her sleep. I couldn't get comfortable, though. The van inched forward, and the sky had grown cloudy, which made the morning feel really dark and slow.

The next thing I knew, drool was slipping from the corner of my mouth.

"How was your nap?" Aaryn asked.

I wiped my mouth and glanced at his shirtsleeve. Thank God. No drool mark that I could tell. I smoothed my hair, which was warmer on my temple from where I'd fallen asleep against his shoulder. I cleared my throat. "Where are we?"

"Almost home," he said.

"What time is it?" I clicked my phone. No new messages, though judging from the party photos Dmitri had posted last night, Danny was probably still in bed.

The brakes made a low squeal as the van slowed, then stopped. No one moved, because moving meant we were finished, we were home, and it was really over. Lakefield. Juliette angled the mirror toward the back and removed her sunglasses. "Well, Aaryn. This has been really great. Thank you. I know things didn't go as planned onstage—but you've helped Karma more than you know."

"Of course," he said. He unbuckled and got out of the van. The seat beside me felt very empty.

"I guess I'll see you around," he said. He was framed in the opening, the fall colors of Lakefield behind him.

I flicked my seat belt off. "I'll be right back." I shimmied out and shut the door without worrying what the girls would think, and then I hugged him, hard, and closed my eyes. "Thank you."

He hugged me back. "Of course. You're welcome."

"I can't remember if I thanked you before."

"You probably did."

I stepped away, my hand reaching for the door, my gaze unable to hold his. "You should come by the studio sometime. I'll be there every night. We have to plan your party."

"Okay." He held on to his bag strap. "When?"

"Anytime. Tomorrow. The next day."

"I will."

The birds were singing, and our van was the only car in sight. "Bye, Aaryn." The door made a grinding sound as it shut. Inside, the air was so stuffy, Aaryn just standing there on the grass, and I was hot and hungry, and sad that it was all over, and sad that I probably wouldn't win.

We drove off. I thought about calling Danny to wake him up—maybe he'd come over—but then I decided that all I wanted to do was get home, where I could be alone and unpack and cry until the depressed feeling in my chest was gone.

CHAPTER 24

AARYN

Day 40

"Hey, Aaryn."

Phoebe. She was relaxed at the top of the stairs when I walked inside my apartment foyer. "Surprise!"

"Yeah. Wow." My foot caught on the step. "Is everything okay?"

"More than okay," she said as I walked up.

I unlocked the door. "After you."

She shrugged out of her quiver and leaned her bow against the wall. "I've missed you." And then she reached through the quiver's opening.

The sound of metal drawn out, clear and bell-like, rang through my apartment. "The assembly doesn't know I'm bringing you this."

The golden arrow burned with light. I held it at arm's length. The blades couldn't get anywhere near my skin. Warmth radiated from the arrow, something I'd never noticed as a god. Now that I was human, the arrow felt so different. Almost alive.

"What is this?" I asked, even though I knew. "I don't understand."

"It's an unmarked arrow." She hesitated. "A universal arrow. Just made. You can shoot Danny with it and no one will know his proposal came as a result. There's no way to track it—no way to know it exists. Once he proposes to her, which shouldn't take long, you can come home. A lot has happened since you left."

I tried to hand it back, but she ignored my offer. "Where did you get this?"

"Somewhere." Her expression became serious. "Trust me, this will work. We won't have to go to Blackout. You do trust me, don't you?"

Flecks of gold danced along the arrow as my hand shook, the glint drawing my eyes to the point. The power to change someone's life forever. I swallowed. "I can't keep this."

"Okay," Phoebe said, laughing a little. Then, realizing I was serious, her smile vanished. "Shoot Danny and come home."

"No, Phoebe. I can't. I cheated once—lied once—and look where it got us."

"Yes." She narrowed her eyes. "Once again, we don't have much of a choice, do we?"

Had she always looked like that? Like I disgusted her if she wasn't in charge? The weight of the arrow felt enormous. I hated it. "An unmarked could be dangerous. What if the formula is wrong? What if it kills him?"

"Would you care?"

"Wow. Yes, I'd *care*, what do you think? I'm not a murderer. Not to mention—Karma would never recover from losing him."

"And I'm supposed to suffer as a result of all of this?" She stepped forward, the glow of her skin making my eyes feel scratchy. "I'm supposed to rot in Blackout, and lose my immortality, because some girl might *cry* a lot?"

The thought of Karma crying filled me with sadness. "We both lied, Phoebe."

Her eyes darkened. "I can't believe we're having this conversation. I thought you cared about me. Anyway, I guess you've decided my fate. Thanks for the info."

"Tek is bringing me a lead arrow to break her enchantment. He's giving you a chip for protection. My father knows." I felt free when I thought of my plan to stay on Earth. Like I could really leave that messed-up world in Olympus behind me.

"*This* arrow is the only way." Her arms relaxed. "I know what Tek said, but we talked everything over and I told him you'd be more than happy to join us once you get home. Chaz and I, Tek, too—we all agreed a golden arrow is the safest bet." Her chin lowered. "You really need to get focused again."

"What do you mean?"

"Focus, Aaryn. Stop worrying about that stupid girl and finish the mission you were sent here to do." She took my hand and closed it around the golden arrow. "You can't decide to cheat one way but not another. Don't be a hypocrite. Come home." She twisted her lips. "We need you there."

"She's not a stupid girl. Far from it. And she'd never dream of asking me to lie or cheat."

"How sweet." Phoebe shrugged. "Everyone is counting on you to finish your mission. Tek's under a lot of pressure from the assembly, your father is—"

"I thought Dad and Tek were working together now."

"Yes," she said quickly.

"I should have told Dad the truth a long time ago."

Phoebe gave a short, cynical laugh. "Why? So you could have gone straight to Blackout like some loser?"

"Tek said he'd give you a chip."

"Yeah, well, no one really knows if that will work."

I placed the golden arrow against the back of the couch. "Tek said he'd be back. He wants me in High Tower, and I told him I won't go without the lead arrow." I did feel like a hypocrite for lying to them.

"A lead arrow is out of the question."

"Why?"

"It's too risky! The assembly could easily run a report that shows her arrow is missing. You know her arrow has already been tracked."

Then one of her dark eyebrows lifted. "Oh my God." She carved her hands through her hair. "Wow. Really—wow. You think you're in love with her, don't you?"

Her knowing the truth was dangerous, but I felt more relaxed than I had in weeks, almost like I'd been subconsciously waiting for the moment when she would know. "I never expected any of this. It just happened."

"Please. You don't love her. You know that, right? It's not like you've been shot."

"I've never felt this way before."

"Obviously. You're human."

"Tell Tek I'm waiting."

She began to shake her head, then shoved by me and gripped the doorknob, her pale mouth a straight line. "Fix your mistake. Don't ruin my life because you think you're in love." She kicked over the bow near the door. "You'll need that, too."

"If you want, you can take my chip."

She was already gone, the door left open. I righted the bow and ran my finger along the silver wire, strong as steel.

I closed the door and sat against it. The golden arrow shimmered on the couch. The wrong arrow. The thought of leaving Karma with Danny, cheating and lying my way back home? That idea left me empty. Maybe that was the point. Maybe I was being punished for interfering with something far more powerful than an arrow's venom . . . human love.

I set the arrow in my closet and slammed the door. Along the bottom, a strip of golden light emanated from within. I flung the door wide and snapped T-shirts from the hangers, bunching the cotton over the arrow to block its light. When I shut the door, the room was black.

The arrow, hidden.

But nothing could block it from my mind.

CHAPTER 25

AARYN

Day 58

The candles in the room flickered as I walked to the door.

"Welcome to my awesome place." With a wave of my arm I stood back, smiling, and Karma seriously looked like she might burst with happiness.

"Wow," she said. "You really went all out." The door at the bottom of the stairs rattled from the wind. My apartment, which I'd scrubbed all day, wasn't the worst dump in the world. At least by candlelight, it looked inviting. She held the baby carrier a few inches forward. "Nice to see you again, stranger."

"It's been a while, huh?"

"Two and a half weeks." She watched me, like she was trying to figure out what was really going on.

"I've been busy." I moved Nell to the middle of the room, making faces, which she loved. She was bundled up in pink from head to toe. "Planning to stay the night?" I joked, meaning the two bags and fuzzy blanket Karma had lugged through the door and piled next to the couch.

"Shut up," Karma said.

I unstrapped Nell, which turned out to be a lot harder than it looked when Karma did it, and tried to hold on to her while wiggling her arms out of her coat. Her boots were pink with fur along the top. Ridiculous, but in a cute way, I guess. She kicked a lot, which made it almost impossible to remove them. "I think she grew since the last time I saw her."

"Babies grow fast," Karma said. "It smells good in here." She glanced around. "How many candles do you *have*?"

"Candles?" Not my fault that tea lights came in packs of a hundred. "Oh, you know. Saves on electricity."

"You might be crossing the line a little there."

"Really? I can blow them out if you're serious. . . ."

I made no attempt, nor had any intention, of blowing them out. I remembered the way she'd looked by candlelight in Milwaukee.

Karma shrugged. "Go green, I guess."

"Go green?"

"Never mind."

She spread out the blanket and knelt beside Nell, who was frantically trying to move and talk at the same time, legs pumping, neck strained. Karma's eyes caught the light, little golden sparks that burned in the center, shadows jumping across her face. "Do you need help with dinner?" she asked.

"I'm all good. Juliette helped me plan a few essentials."

"Essentials? Like what?"

"A salad with lots of healthy, dancer-type stuff, and cheesy bread. She said the salad would impress you and the cheesy bread would be a guilty pleasure."

"Oh my God, she said that?"

"She did."

"I had no idea you talked to her about this."

"Every man has his secrets." I sat on the opposite side of the blanket, which felt really safe and really dangerous at the same time. Karma was wearing a tight black dress, leggings, and tall boots. She'd obviously done her hair, which was down, the curls prettier than normal, tendrils framing her face.

"What?" she said.

"Nothing."

"Why are you looking at me like that?"

"You're beautiful," I said.

"Oh. Thanks." She stood and began wandering around the room. "Do you have any music?"

I dug my phone out of my pocket. "What are you in the mood for?"

"How about the Black Keys?"

"Okay."

The timer went off on the stove at the same moment the drums kicked in.

"Let's take this party to the table," I said. "I'll be right back."

The oven creaked open with a blast of heat, filling the air with the scent of butter and cheese. I fumbled to plate the salad, lost a few strawberries in the process, and rounded the corner with a pounding heart.

"For our first course," I said, "a strawberry walnut salad with grilled chicken and a champagne vinaigrette."

"Impressive." She moved Nell beside her on the blanket,

shaking a toy above her daughter's outstretched hands. "That's a pretty fancy salad."

I sat in the chair across from her and stared until she took a bite. I leaned forward a little.

"Is it good?" I asked.

"So good." She licked the tip of her fork. "I love salad."

"That's what Juliette said." I sounded way too eager.

She chewed thoughtfully, then swallowed and set down her fork. "I've decided how I'm going to use the scholarship money if I get it."

I twisted the end of my fork against the lettuce. "Oh?"

She reached for one of the glasses of water I'd set out. "There's a dance program at the University of Southern Mississippi, which is about a two-and-a-half-hour drive from Danny's school."

"That seems far," I said. "How are you going to take care of Nell all alone like that?"

"Two and a half hours is a lot better than twenty. Danny and I will still be able to see each other every weekend. If things *don't* work out with the scholarship, maybe I can apply for a grant." Her smile had definitely faded. "Or there's always financial aid."

"What about New York?"

She gave a little head shake. "That's not going to work."

"You haven't cancelled your admission yet, have you?" If she waited until Tek got back to me, her plan would definitely change.

She smoothed her hair behind her ear. "It's on my to-do list."

"Is that really what you want? To be in Mississippi by yourself, no support, just so you'll be eighteen hours closer to Danny?"

She stabbed the greens on her plate over and over. "Of course that's what I want."

"Is that what *he* wants?"

"He said he wanted us to go with him." Her tone was verging on angry, which was how it always seemed whenever he was the topic of conversation.

While she shoved a forkful of salad into her mouth, I raised my glass. "Okay. To the future." After a few seconds she lifted her glass.

"To the future."

There was sadness where there should have been excitement. Our glasses clinked. We finished our first course to the welcome racket of the rock music. I really thought Tek would have come by now—that Phoebe would have talked to him, set things straight. I had to get that lead arrow before she called New York. I didn't feel hungry, but I kept eating.

"So good," she repeated when she was done. Then her eyes widened and she dug my bucket list out of one of the bags she'd brought. "We have to cross this off. Here, you do the honors."

I drew a black line through the words, though I couldn't stop thinking about how everything on the napkin had been an excuse to spend more time with her. Two and a half weeks apart. Too long. The list was already getting short. "Let me grab the second course."

In the kitchen I lined up the plates until they were exactly straight and placed a piece of cheesy bread in the center for each of us. Before I rounded the corner, Nell had started to fuss.

"Oh, baby," Karma crooned. She shook the toy and nodded at the plate I set before her. "I like my cheese a little brown on top, too."

"I know."

"You did not."

I just smiled mysteriously. Nell broke out in a full-on fit.

"Little babe!" Karma patted her back and smelled her butt, which seemed to pass the test, but Nell wasn't getting any happier. "I just fed her, but let me try again."

A ten-minute ordeal of forcing a bottle into her mouth, having her choke and cry, Karma burping her, rocking her from one side of her body to the next—none of it worked.

"Let's go for a walk, like in Milwaukee," I suggested.

"Oh, no, that's okay."

Nell's cry sounded madder by the second. "Let's just try it," I said, moving toward the door.

"I don't want to."

"She'll love it."

And then I saw the fear in her eyes.

"I don't want anyone to get the wrong idea about us," Karma said. She was trying really hard to make the explanation sound normal.

"Doesn't Danny know we had this planned?"

"No." Her face was stricken, Nell screaming in her ear. "He's with Dmitri."

"Have you guys talked about Mississippi?"

"Of course we have."

I paused. "Karma. I don't mean to be a jerk, but I have to say something. You're giving up your whole future for a guy you can't even be real with."

"If you want to be my friend, you have to stop doing that," she said quietly.

"Doing what?"

"Talking bad about Danny. I love him, and it hurts when you say things like that. It makes being your friend really hard."

"Then why are you even here?"

"Because I'm lonely!"

Nell stuffed her fist into her mouth, almost as if she was soothed by the sound of her mother's outburst. Karma hugged her baby close. "I'm lonely, and I can't stay away from you."

I didn't dare move. Didn't dare erase the space between us.

Karma's posture softened as she closed her eyes. "I don't know why. I don't even have an excuse, but I can't stay away. You make me feel important, and happy, and I don't know."

"You are important to me." I swallowed. "I'm sorry I haven't been around. I'm trying to get everything in place so I can come back to Lakefield. Remember?"

"I'm not even that nice to you."

"You're everything to me."

She blinked and sighed the longest sigh possible. My pulse was racing, so it was a good thing when she tipped Nell onto her back in her arms. "She's asleep."

"Do you want to lay her down in my room for a while?"

"Do you have some pillows I can set up around her?"

I nodded and we tiptoed to my room.

The golden arrow was in the closet, hidden, of course, but still. Nell didn't wake when Karma eased her onto my comforter, and we crept out of the room.

"Yes!" she exclaimed when we were back at the table. She smashed a high five against my hand. "Sometimes she's impossible to put down, then all of a sudden she's out."

I closed my fingers around her hand. "Dance with me." She started to pull away, but I held firm. "I know this is crossing the line." We stood in the middle of the room, candles everywhere. "I want to dance with you alone, right now, no judges, no competitors. Just us."

Karma hesitated. "You make it sound like this is our last dance or something. We still have to plan your going-away party. You're coming back in what, three months?" We both seemed happier when she said it.

"We won't be able to dance at the party." I placed my other hand on her waist. "And it will be a while after that." *Maybe never.*

"I don't know why you're only moving for three months. That's stupid."

I held her hand high and she spun slowly. "You'll have to trust me when I tell you that I don't have a choice."

"Are you a criminal?"

"No."

"Are you in trouble?"

"Not really." I swallowed, because I didn't feel like lying to her about my past when she was so close to being in my arms.

"If things work out—will you come with me when I get my tattoo?" I asked.

"You're not serious about that, are you? *Lakefield, Wisconsin?*"

"I never want to forget this place." I released her long enough to switch the song to something slower. Acoustic folk. When I took her hand and waist and pressed her against me, the protest that had to be at the tip of her tongue wasn't spoken. The music played, a love song, and for a while we just danced, touching where we could, me being careful not to cross the line any further than I already had. We understood each other when we danced. Our bodies just fit together.

"You'll really be gone three months?" she asked.

"Yes." I eased her in front of me, where she took five steps and seemed really content. She always looked like that when she was dancing. "I'll call you," I added.

"This whole idea is weird. No hearts around the Lakefield tat, whatever you do."

"Just a few?"

She laughed, which was how I always wanted her to be. Happy, in my arms, feeling important. All the places we touched felt amazing. "I'll give you a letter," I said. "When I get back, I want you to give it to me. I don't want to forget anything about our time together."

"Here I thought it wasn't possible for this idea to get any weirder. I was wrong."

"You'll be leaving me, too, you know." I rubbed my thumb across her lower back. "Going to school. Following your dreams."

She swayed with me and didn't speak, but when she fit her hands behind my neck and rested her cheek against my shoulder, I swear she whispered, "Shhh."

CHAPTER 26

KARMA

With a teensy bit of nagging, we'd set a date for his going-away party: Saturday night, two weeks after our dinner, complete with a bonfire and strands of twinkly lights. Peyton helped me decorate.

"Wow, Karma, you're really going all out." She stood on a ladder, holding a roll of red streamers that matched her hair.

I finished twirling the strand into a perfect coil, cut the end, and taped it to the corner of the ceiling. The middle hung in a glorious arc. "I just wanted to do something nice for him after everything he's done for me."

"When is he leaving?"

"Sixteen days."

"Wow, you even know the number of days."

"He's pretty precise with his timing." I climbed down and positioned my stepladder a few feet forward. The tape dispenser clattered to the floor. "Do you think it's weird that Danny refuses to come to the party?" I grabbed the tape and tore four pieces along the serrated edge.

"Not really." Peyton skipped forward, the ladder scraping the floor. "He hates Aaryn, right? I'd be more surprised if he *came.*"

"I don't think he *hates* him. The fight was a long time ago. They're over it, I'm sure."

"Karma." Peyton tugged the streamer. It stretched to the point of tearing, then relaxed. "They both like you. That's why Danny doesn't want to come. Too much testosterone in one room."

"Aaryn doesn't like me in that way. He's just a friend. A really nice guy—you said so yourself."

"Mm-hmm."

"Don't act like that." I tore the streamer until it floated from her grasp. She pretended to be appalled. "Don't make things awkward between me and Aaryn. Please?"

"You're the one interpreting it that way."

"You're impossible."

"So are you."

"Let's blow up the balloons." At least with a balloon in her mouth she couldn't make her observational comments. For a few seconds, the only sound in the studio was rubber expanding with our breaths.

"What's with all the gray?" Peyton asked, bumping my head with a balloon.

"Aaryn claims it's his favorite color." I made a face. "I told him that's boring and that I was adding red to the room to liven things up."

"Huh. Weirdo."

"Right?" My half-blown balloon deflated as Danny's truck skidded into the driveway. Not again. Not now.

"Speak of the devil," Peyton mumbled.

Danny stood at the screen door wearing a cut-off tee and

jeans with holes in the knees. His hat was cocked off one side of his head. Messy but cute.

"I thought you weren't coming." I held my hand to the screen, smiling a little when his touched from the other side.

"Can I come in?"

The hinges creaked as I opened the door. He shuffled inside and crossed his arms as he surveyed the room. "Heh. Guess he's pretty special."

"It's just a few streamers. All the girls are helping."

He kicked the balloon Peyton had just finished. It made a loud thunk as it skidded across the floor. "At least now I know why you've been so busy."

Peyton eyed me, a balloon in her mouth. I turned and gave Danny a serious look.

"Let's talk outside."

I led the way, and to be honest, a little bit of guilt stabbed me. I *had* been busy, and yeah, I'd been messaging Aaryn about the party, but we hadn't seen each other since dinner.

Dinner.

I climbed into the truck with a heavy heart. Danny slammed the door and leaned back with a shrug, snorting a little to clear his nose.

"Can you say something?" I sat cross-legged on the seat. The truck smelled like cigarettes and dirty shoes, a bunch of dried mud pieces covering the floor mats. "Come to the party. I want you to be there. I definitely don't want any of this to be weird." I slid my hand over his arm. "I love you."

He fixed his hat, brushing away my touch. "You know how I feel about that guy, yet you insist on doing shit like this for him."

"I know, and I'm sorry, but he's really been there for me

with the scholarship and stuff." I glanced out the window. Noon already. There was still a lot to do. It was a sunny fall day, gusty winds, but it was really quiet inside the truck. "I don't want to feel like I'm hiding things. So."

"Hiding things?"

I turned, sliding my hands over my knees. "I saw Aaryn two weeks ago. He made dinner, and Nell and I stopped by his apartment for a while. Also, I've been talking to him about the party, but that's it. I swear. This doesn't have to come between us. He's paying for the party, and everyone at Shining Waters is helping put it together, not just me."

Danny's mouth twisted into a sneer. "When did you become such a slut?"

And the air just left me, left me empty, a girl in a lotus pose in a stuffy truck. "I'm not cheating on you."

"Yeah, like I can believe anything you say."

"Please come. The party will be fun. We're having a bonfire, making s'mores, everything. Mom and Leah will be there, Nick, too. I want you there with me."

Danny chuckled sarcastically. "You don't need me." He turned the key. "Get out."

"Don't leave mad. We have to trust each other. I love you."

"Get. Out."

My foot barely touched gravel before he sped off. I gulped back tears, cutting tears, suffocating tears. He was a jerk, but I couldn't help feeling that maybe I deserved his anger, a little at least. Maybe if I'd told the truth up front, instead of hiding my plans, he wouldn't be so upset.

I wiped my face hard and sniffed as I dried my hands on my shirt.

CHAPTER 27

AARYN

Day 74

The pen left a tiny blue dot on each date as I counted.

Monday. I circled it. Day 90 would fall on a Monday, a regular, stupid Monday to either fail my mission or cheat, depending on if Tek ever got back to me. I'd decided something.

And I wrote the letter.

To Aaryn.

I drew a line through my name because it might change in Blackout, who knows, and because it wasn't a part of the letter that mattered. Slowly I started over:

To the guy with Lakefield, Wisconsin, tattooed on his arm.

You're probably wondering why Karma seems to know you.
Look up. Your whole world is here.

Yes. It's right there with her, the girl who gave you the letter. This letter is all you need to know for now. Don't skim.

I could try to explain how you lost your memory, but that's really weird, and probably too confusing to understand right now. I'll just get to the important part. Wait, are you paying attention? Because if there's one thing you must not do, not now, not ever, it's lose her.

You should let her know right now how beautiful she is.

Stop overthinking things. Stop thinking this letter is crazy, and tell her, right now, that you can't wait to spend time with her.

Look up.

Don't lose her. Do not lose her.

Ask her to dance with you. Write a new bucket list and cross something off today. Ask her to tell you everything she remembers. She seems like a stranger, but if you wait a week—hell, it might only take a day—I swear you will know how special she is. You cannot lose her now. You will know that she's worth all the confusion you're feeling.

You fell for her once, and you will again.

Take a chance.

The paper felt smooth as I folded it into three even sections. I placed it in my closet next to the golden arrow, my other option for fixing Karma's life. Because if Day 90 came without Tek, no matter how much it hurt, I'd do it. That's what I'd decided.

I'd shoot Danny with the golden arrow; yes, it would kill me, really kill me—but I'd wait in the school parking lot with the golden arrow until Danny walked out. I'd fix things for her one way or the other.

A horn beeped twice. Karma was waiting downstairs.

CHAPTER 28

KARMA

The studio had this amazing vibe when we walked in, like I'd really pulled off a night to remember with all the balloons and music and just the right amount of red.

Aaryn. "This looks great." His eyes were lit by just the right amount of twinkle. "Thanks."

"Sure." I felt like bursting.

Peyton made her way over with Nell on her hip, Nick trailing behind. "You have to try your mom's dip." She had a smear of something cheesy on the side of her mouth.

"Honey, look at me," Nick said. He used a napkin to wipe her face, crumpled it, and stuck his hand out to Aaryn. "Happy going away, man. Lakefield won't be the same without you."

Aaryn shook his hand, but he didn't seem to like being reminded of the reason we were all here. I stole my baby from Peyton's arms and kissed her cheek. "I'm starving. Come on, Aaryn, I'll show you everything."

The sun was setting, though it was unseasonably warm for mid-November. Still no snow, but we'd all need jackets for the bonfire.

"I didn't know I had so many friends," Aaryn confided.

I smiled. The girls of Shining Waters had invited people from town, so it really seemed like we had a good turnout. Svetlana had her arm around a boy. I held Nell on my hip and felt a little rush of pride at how delicious everything looked. "Let's eat."

We filled our plates with the pulled pork Mom had made, the dip, Juliette's fruit salad, chips, appetizers, and pickles galore.

"What are those yellow things?" Aaryn pointed to a small glass plate.

"Fresh cheese curds. The fresher they are, the more they squeak."

He tried one, the squeaking sound audible with every bite. "I feel weird." He chewed. "And I'm eating cheese that squeaks."

I laughed. Leah waved at us and patted the table next to the windows. She, Mom, and Juliette were poised to pounce. Aaryn and I sat down.

"Aaryn, so nice to finally meet you," Mom said. "I've heard so much about you already, all good. Thank you so much for everything you've done to help my girl."

"It was my pleasure," Aaryn said.

"Did she tell you about the cake for her announcement?"

He nudged my side. "Announcement?"

"Just a little something I have planned for later. You'll see."

Leah wiggled her eyebrows at me, though thankfully I didn't think Aaryn noticed. I made a calculated attempt to kick her but connected with the table leg instead.

"Whoops," I said.

"It's so sad that you're leaving," Leah crooned. She scooted to angle toward him and sat with her chin in her hand.

"I really like Lakefield," Aaryn said. "You were right, what you said about it being a small town full of good people," he told Juliette.

"Ah, so you've noticed." My aunt's mouth lifted into a small, sort of sad smile. "I came here a long time ago to be with the love of my life but found a new love instead—this place." She gestured toward the room. It struck me suddenly that both my aunt and my mother had fallen for these tragic loves, two men who hadn't turned out to be what they thought. Mom tugged Nell's hand, which was wrapped tight around her finger, smiling and talking to her. They were both amazing in different ways. Both really strong.

"When do you think we should start the bonfire?" I asked. "The wind's died down. Maybe soon?"

"We can get it going after dinner," Mom said.

We chatted about regular, safe things for the rest of dinner, Aaryn rehashing the details of his leaving for the tenth time, me feeling both sad and satisfied at the way the night was going. I wasn't obsessing about Danny. Not really. Yes, he would have had a good time with us, but I couldn't make him like Aaryn, and I couldn't make him understand how important the party was to me.

An hour later, when we were full and tired from small talk, Aaryn and I decided to go outside. Nell had fallen asleep next to Mom. The cold November wind crept through my clothes, the way it always did, even though I wore a winter jacket. I hugged myself and rubbed my arms to stay warm.

"A little different from Florida, huh?" I said. The fire roared and snapped, and we stood close to it. There were other kids around I recognized from school. I smiled and offered a polite hi.

The fire felt soothing. I held my hands out, drawn to the flames, staring and staring.

"I wonder if it will snow before I leave," Aaryn said. He was turning his hands in the light, shadows around them. The scent of woodsmoke bit back against the chill.

"I hope so. You should experience snow at least once."

"I always thought it was cool to look at."

"Give it five months and then get back to me."

We smiled, entranced—entranced by the fire and everything that was between us. He was a good friend, a good dance partner, and even though he wasn't leaving for another sixteen days, suddenly the night really felt like goodbye.

"You're really leaving," I said.

"Yes."

"But you'll be back. You still have to get that tattoo." I nudged him. "And the letter. You said you'd write me one."

"I have it at home. But, Karma—things have changed a little."

"Changed?"

"I just, I don't know if I'll be able to come back, or if any of that, the letter, the tattoo, I just don't know if any of that will matter." The firewood collapsed, sending a spray of sparks into the sky.

"Oh."

"Let's just enjoy tonight." He took my hand and squeezed, then let it go again. "This is a great party. Can we do that?"

"Sure."

But there was sadness now, and a mood I couldn't figure out. I couldn't pinpoint the emotion for it. Regret and guilt and uncertainty all in one.

I lost my footing when Leah grabbed me. "I have to tell you something," she said. "Now." Her voice came through her teeth. We walked off and Aaryn started to follow, but Leah waved him away, and soon we were just cold, just us sisters standing at the side of the studio. She was really upset about something.

"You won't believe what I just found out." I opened my mouth to ask, "What?" but she had her hands around mine, tight. "Danny and Jen have been hooking up. I just talked to Megan, who was at the shack just now, where Danny and Jen happened to be, and she said she saw them, you know, *saw them* in his truck. I'm going to kill him. Karma, I'm seriously going to hurt that creep for doing this to you. I knew something was up with him, I just knew it."

"Wait, what? Who?" The wind blew, but this time the cold felt good. The cold helped me think.

"Danny's been sneaking around with Jen for *months*, ugh, I could murder them both."

"Stop talking like that."

"Well, I could."

"I need to talk to Danny."

"I agree. I think you should drive over there right now and confront them both."

"I don't want drama."

"Come on, Karma—get pissed!" My sister shook me, my teeth chattering. "Go yell at him as loud as you can. Tell him he's a creep."

"We need to talk. I don't know. Are you sure Megan knows what she saw?"

Leah made an outrageous face. "Really? You can't believe your boyfriend, who is a complete asshole, would cheat on you again? My God, get a clue."

"Why are you being so mean?" Tears flooded my eyes and inside I felt sick, like I might fall apart. Leah's mad face softened a little. She sighed loudly and crushed me in a hug. I was frozen. I was dying.

"What's going on?" Aaryn blocked my view of the fire. Leah waited for me to answer, but I couldn't. I couldn't speak when I was that close to dying. She shrugged and placed Aaryn's hand on my shoulder.

"Danny cheated. Try to talk some sense into her." Then she stomped off.

Aaryn's worried look was only making me sicker, making me want to throw up. "What's going on? Is she serious?"

Leah knew, everyone *knew*. Even Aaryn.

I shook my head and turned away when he placed his hand on my arm, and the fire blurred into a big yellow ball.

CHAPTER 29

AARYN

Day 74

"What are you going to do?" I asked, slowing to a stop. I turned toward my apartment, the blinker ticking into the silence.

Karma sat in the passenger seat with her phone in her lap. "I have to call him," she said. "Maybe—" She faced me, her eyes wide despite the tears in them. "Maybe it's just a rumor. You know how things are in a small town. I guess I just really need to talk to Danny."

"Okay."

"Leah hates him. She's always looking for ways to make him look bad."

"Hmmm." We pulled up to my apartment and sat there for a while.

"I'll call him upstairs," she said. She was still stunning in her oversized jacket, that loose, messy hair, and a selfish part of me almost wanted the rumor to be true so she'd hug me. Need me.

I unlocked the door with a weird anticipation in my stomach, but mostly I just felt like a jerk.

She made the call right in my living room. I stood there waiting but not looking at her, because it seemed really wrong to anticipate any sort of pain in her reaction.

"Danny?" She cupped her hands over the phone. "Hey. It's me. Where are you right now?" She plugged her left ear. I could hear loud music in the background, even though the call wasn't on speaker. "Can you go somewhere quieter?"

She looked so sad. "Have you heard the rumor people are spreading about you and Jen?" Her fingers turned white as she gripped the phone, listening. "Mm-hmm. Leah said her friend Megan said you two have been sleeping together." She waited but then whipped the phone from her ear in shock. "He hung up on me."

"Wow."

"I can't believe this. I can't believe this is happening again."

"So he cheated?"

"He hung up! That's practically like admitting it, right?"

"I don't know. Seems pretty sketchy."

"Why is he doing this to me?"

"I have no idea."

"He knows I'm applying to Southern Miss. I can't believe this. He said he wanted us to go with him."

"I'm sorry." After a second of hesitation, I pushed away from the wall and stood next to her.

"I can't go through this again." Her voice had a desperate, breathy sound, like she was on the verge of hyperventilating. "I can't stay with him and wonder if this is true or if he'll cheat again—it drives me crazy. I can't do it and I won't. You have to help me."

"How?"

"I don't know. I guess I need to know the fucking truth!" The light above us shadowed her eyes, her lips, her collarbone. "What's wrong with me? I mean, what! Am I ugly? Am I a bad girlfriend? Am I stupid?"

I took an immediate step forward and leaned down, firm hands catching her waist.

I kissed her.

Silenced her.

I wasn't breathing anymore, or worrying, or thinking about anything except her taste.

Her lips soft beneath mine.

The kiss had trapped her hand against my chest, making it easy, so easy, to push me away.

But she didn't.

I felt her hair and she melted toward me, toward me and not away. With a long inhale, I lifted her up with my arm against her back until she was edged against the wall. I pulled away, my mouth wet, her eyes still closed.

"You're beautiful," I said. "You're talented and sweet and smart, and the most amazing person I've ever met. I don't know why he cheats. He doesn't deserve you."

She started crying again.

"Sorry," I said, stepping back a little. "Don't cry. Say something."

"I'm trying."

She sounded so pathetic, a lump rose in my throat.

"Are you mad?" I said.

"No. I . . . I'm thinking." She turned away fast and jammed her knuckles over her tears. "Maybe he didn't cheat."

"Karma. Look at me."

She did, her cheeks blotchy and wet.

"Tell me I'm not imagining this," I said. "Don't you feel it? There's something between us. There always has been. What are you feeling?"

I felt like I'd been running. She stared, unblinking, almost as if she couldn't focus on me. The arrow was still making her miserable. Still making her want him.

"I don't know what I feel anymore," she said with a shrug.

"Well, you mean a lot to me. I want to be with you all the time."

"You'd be better off kissing someone who deserves you."

I shook my head. "You're the only one I want."

She couldn't help a little smile, which changed into a frown seconds later when her phone rang. "Hey, Leah."

I watched as she listened, then took a deep breath.

"No, keep going," she said. She turned and sat on the couch, then stretched out, like she couldn't hold herself up any longer. Her breathing was erratic. "Oh my God," she whispered. "No. Tell me. I want to know . . . this is tearing me apart."

There was nothing I could say to comfort her, though there were a million heartless words at the tip of my tongue.

Ditch the loser.

He's never loved you.

I could love you better.

But the arrow.

She ended the call. Her shoulders shook as she cried. I knelt guiltily beside her, sighing as she collapsed against me. "Can I get you anything?"

She sniffed loudly, her face wet, eyes bloodshot. Her gaze on me was pitiful as she curled around a couch cushion, letting her face rest against the tweed, sloppy. Our faces were inches apart, but there was nothing sexy about our gaze now, not when she cried.

"What did Leah say?"

The life had left her eyes. She shook her head fast, as if telling me would kill her.

"I'm sorry," I said.

She didn't know the number of things I regretted. I could add one more to the list: the golden arrow shoved in the back of my closet. If I'd shot Danny right away, like Phoebe had wanted, I might have helped Karma avoid her pain. Once again I was too late.

CHAPTER 30

KARMA

"I'm not *at* home, Danny." I slid my phone to the other side of my hair. "I'm at Aaryn's apartment." A stupid part of me longed for him to care. I felt a little stronger after my cry. A little like I was ready to break something instead of break down.

"Babe, Prodigy, I'm going to pick you up. We can talk, okay? I'm leaving now."

I reached noisily for a tissue. "No. You lied to me again. *You* did this to our family. I'm done covering for you, and paying for you, and supporting Nell by myself, and being your fool." I stopped to avoid crying. *You love him.*

I hated myself.

The scent of coffee from the kitchen only hurt more. Why couldn't Danny be more like that? Why couldn't he be there for me when I needed him most?

"Babe, I know I screwed up."

"You think?"

"You're the only girl I want. You and Nell, my two girls. I'm leaving now, okay?"

I scoffed. The flutter in my stomach hearing him beg. I knew it wasn't healthy. "Only girl? Ha." My crumpled tissue bounced lightly off the wastebasket next to the bathroom sink. "Did you really think you could go around sleeping with Jen and who knows who else without me knowing? You are an idiot. The biggest idiot I've ever met." I used volume to emphasize the *idiot*s. I tried not to feel bad for yelling at him.

"I swear this is the last time, Karma. You're right, I am an idiot. Please, I have to see you. We can work this out."

"You don't deserve to see me or touch me or talk to me ever again."

I rolled my eyes as he continued to beg, set the phone on the sink, and began fixing my hair in the mirror. When his stupid voice was no longer begging from the phone, I picked it up.

"I don't want to see you tonight or ever," I said. "We're through. So goodbye."

I punched the end button and doubled over until the sharp pain in my stomach faded. My phone lit up a second later. The buzzing made me want to scream. I marched out of the bathroom with my finger on the ignore call button. Aaryn had spread a blanket over the couch and was reading on top of it, his head against the armrest. He glanced up.

"Do you want to talk about it?"

"No." I ended another attempted call from Danny and sat on the opposite side of the couch. "I just want to punch him or die, I don't know."

"I had no idea you could yell like that. Remind me not to get on your bad side."

"I'm not in the mood for jokes."

"I know. Sorry."

The phone in my hand would not shut up. I groaned. "Do you care if I take this in your bedroom? I'm not feeling the greatest. I think I need to lie down."

"Go ahead."

"Are you sure you don't mind?"

"Not at all."

I shuffled into his bedroom and shut the door. His room was simple, no-fuss, and I didn't think twice about crawling into his bed, the sheets that smelled like him, a hint of cologne, his bitter soap. My eyes closed and the burning feeling disappeared. I felt like all my tears had left me empty, not even a person, just a shell with nothing inside, lost in a great lake. I felt hot, feverish, even, and the pain in my stomach had gotten worse.

When Danny's number popped up moments later, I realized I'd been holding my breath. Fear had crept into my chest, a horrible black ink. I pushed answer and held the phone to my ear.

"Karma, please."

My eyes eased shut when I heard his voice. He still wanted me. And despite everything, despite how angry and hurt I was, I just wasn't ready to let him go. My tears came again, slow, wet droplets streaming down to soak Aaryn's pillow.

I cried in silence as Danny promised me all sorts of things, things I knew deep in my heart would never come true. The release felt like waves over my body, and the sound of his voice was like a spring, helping me forgive, forget.

CHAPTER 31

AARYN

Day 74

The doorknob to my bedroom turned, and Karma came out, eyes puffier than when she went in, hair disheveled, like a girl who'd been beaten. Her cheeks were unnaturally red.

"Are you okay?" I asked. She wouldn't look at me. "What did he say? What's going on?"

She picked up her purse from the couch, the leather sliding against her hip. "I'm going to go."

"What? But—did you talk about things? From the way you were yelling, it seemed like you were going to break up."

I followed her as she took a few more steps toward the door. She hugged the purse. "No."

"No?"

The zipper made a scratching sound as she opened it, then dropped her phone inside. "Can you just—stop worrying about this? I know he's an ass, but he said he's sorry and there's just a lot you don't understand." Her bottom lip quivered when she finished.

"I do understand." I tried to pull her toward me for a hug, but she stiffened. "Karma." I smoothed her hair behind her ear. The curls were a little damp from her tears. "I understand more than you know."

She was so pitiful and strong at the same time, fighting a power she didn't even realize controlled her. My arrow. My arrow had turned her into this. I stood in front of her, my hands on her arms. She was shaking her head.

"You don't," she whispered. "You couldn't." Her hands pressed against her stomach, her frown deepening.

"You need to lie down."

"No. I'm fine. I think I'm just sore from dancing."

"We have to talk. I don't even know how to start."

"Danny's on his way over." She slid away from my touch, the kitchen linoleum creaking as she walked to the sink. The water sprayed into her glass.

"He is? Why are you going with *him*?"

She finished the water and placed the glass on the counter. "We have a lot going on between us right now."

My breathing was really shaky. "And that's what you want? To go with him?"

"Yes." She dug around in her purse, then typed a message on her phone, mouth set in a line.

"Don't go. Don't go with him, not now."

"I have to."

"What if I told you there was a way to stop feeling like this?"

She stood there for many moments, then strode toward the door.

"Hey, I'm serious," I said. "I know you feel like you have to stay with him, but I swear—"

"Can you please stop talking?" She gasped and bent in half. Great. I'd made her cry again. She breathed in hard, but her nose was all clogged.

"Stay with me." I stepped closer. "We can have coffee. I'll explain everything. I'll tell you everything. I promise."

She closed her eyes slowly and just stood there, not moving, not speaking.

Her phone buzzed.

"I really have to go."

The sound of the door closing behind her felt like a gunshot. Something inside of me broke in that moment, my ego, maybe, my heart.

My fists had closed, the veins rising along the top. I ran to the bedroom and opened the closet with a bang. I threw the T-shirts off the golden arrow and grabbed the shaft. The blades brushed my arm—fine. Maybe it could ruin my life next. I snatched the bow, feeling the cool curved handle, wire that pinged when my fingertip brushed the edge.

Running, the stairs didn't take long. Not when I felt so much rage. In the darkness I immediately spotted where Danny had parked in front of the apartment. It had started to rain, a cold autumn rain that would soon change into snow. The droplets stung my face, my ragged breath making a cloud before me into the night. A small shrub hid my presence, but I saw him clearly: Danny's silhouette through the branches. He talked while his hands gestured in sweeping motions. He was the one she wanted.

I fit the arrow into the bow and pulled, the string making

a slicing sound, metal on metal, a sound that was familiar and nauseating. I hadn't changed much as a human. I was still willing to cheat and lie my way out of trouble. What did I care about love? She wanted him.

His face was right there.

Right in my sights.

My shot would change everything.

As soon as he proposed I would go home.

I closed one eye and stared, my body hot with adrenaline. The moment had come. I saw him as if I had a telescope, his face was so clear, the words he spoke almost audible.

My arm didn't tire of holding the arrow toward him, and my breathing had returned to normal, calm, ready.

He punched the dashboard.

My eyelid twitched.

He did it again, again. His fist pounded the plastic, the veins in his neck protruding, yelling at her. He was no longer sorry. He'd never been sorry, not before, not now. I couldn't do it. She deserved to choose who she loved.

Just as I was going to relax my arm, someone reached around my stomach. A face pressed into the middle of my back. Soft, slender fingers slipped over my hand, guiding the arrow's grip.

With a snap, the arrow flew. It landed on Danny with a burst of light, the perfect shot. I waited, not breathing as I watched Danny's silhouette.

He wasn't yelling anymore.

I whirled around. "Phoebe!"

"Finally." Her emerald eyes flickered. "Nice shot."

I hurled the bow against the building. It clanged noisily. "Why did you sneak up on me like that? My God, what have we done?" In the truck Karma and Danny talked calmly. My throat hurt from the tight feeling surrounding it.

"You were aiming right at him," Phoebe said.

"I was angry." The aura around her pulsed. "I wasn't going to shoot."

"Now we just have to wait for the proposal," Phoebe said. "Too bad you'll have to stay until then."

"I'd rather die than wait for that."

She sighed and reached to comfort me, one glowing hand against my arm. "It's not so bad, really. Soon you'll be home. We've waited a long time for this."

I shrugged away from her touch. "We?"

Phoebe lifted her palms skyward, the light from her hands illuminating her face even more. "Don't you get it? There's still a life for you on Olympus. I know, you're mad you can't be with Karma, poor you, but the truth is I just saved your life. Now you can come home. Be back where you're supposed to be."

"I was going to go to Blackout. Like I should have at finals."

"What?"

"I wasn't going to join Tek. I was going to fix my mistake. Break Karma's enchantment with the lead arrow, if it ever got here. Fail my mission. Go to Blackout."

"And what, be mortal?"

"Yes."

Phoebe gave a short laugh. "This girl has really messed you up. You're being totally irrational."

"We were going to find each other after Blackout."

"Uh-huh."

"I don't know if it would have worked." I met her eyes. "Maybe it was a crazy idea, but it was the best I could think of. She could have loved me. We could have started over, together." My hands were beginning to feel numb.

"You'd rather be human?" Phoebe looked incredulous.

"Maybe."

She rolled her eyes. "Well, okay—you're welcome. Now you can't be stupid. I have to get back. See you after he proposes."

"I don't want to wait." I stepped toward her. "I can't stay for that. I can't."

"Until he proposes, the assembly won't believe your mission is complete. There's no choice but to wait. I told you, no one can find out about the golden arrow, okay?" She shook her head. "See you soon." With a wave of her hand she flickered and disappeared.

The stairs to my apartment creaked with each step forward. It didn't seem possible to feel lost inside a narrow stairwell, but that night I did.

Tek's chip was on the table. I locked the door behind me with a click. It was time to push all the lies into the open, no matter what the consequence. It was time to make sure that what happened to Karma never happened again.

I placed the square chip into my palm, then sucked air, hard. Fear pricked my skin as I drew the chip to my mouth.

CHAPTER 32

KARMA

"How could you leave the party with him?" Danny shook his head and punched the dashboard of his truck.

I flinched. The engine was noisy, glugging gas. I was quiet for a while, then took a deep breath and placed my folded hands on my lap. "How could you cheat?" I clutched the sides of my stomach and leaned forward, feeling like I might vomit. Maybe the stench of smoke had something to do with how nauseated I felt. "I mean, seriously, are you saying that because I go somewhere with my friend, it's okay for you to cheat? I thought you were coming here so we could talk, and obviously we have a *lot* to talk about, but I'm really, really tired of the conversation."

"Oh, this is great, just so typical, you acting like you're better than me, you and your perfect family."

The gnawing pains in my belly, pains I'd only experienced during childbirth, made it hard to focus. "What? This has nothing to do with my family."

"Yeah, you're just so perfect, aren't you?" His fist landed on the dashboard with a crack. "Maybe if your dad hadn't run off, you wouldn't be such a slut. Do you think? Huh?" *Thump.*

Thump.

I cowered against the door.

Then a breeze.

A change.

Danny's face.

The anger lines in his forehead and eyebrows had softened and his shoulders relaxed. "Karma," he said, leaning toward me. Was he going to kiss me?

Despite the fact that every muscle in my body throbbed with pain, I turned my face, barely avoiding his thick lips. "Just— don't touch me, okay?" I didn't want his lips. He'd lied to me so many times. Hurt me. I deserved better, and so did Nell.

I wanted better.

The pain inside me began to fade. It recoiled, as if being wound on a music box. With each second that I admitted the truth to myself, a release spread over my torso, little sparks, little stings. I gasped and grabbed the seat for support. What was happening to me? The feeling was both sad and beautiful, sad because of the truth and beautiful from the freedom it told. My body no longer felt heavy. The nausea that had sickened me for weeks lightened, then disappeared. I turned to the window, to the shadowy outline of trees and buildings. Mist floated along the ground.

"Don't touch me," I whispered.

"Babe, I'm so sorry. I love you." His voice was soft and desperate. Unfamiliar. He covered my hand with his, but I felt nothing. I pulled mine away.

"I'm going to make this right," he continued. "First, dinner like I promised." He dragged the gear back and began to drive toward the highway.

"Dinner won't fix what you've done."

"Marry me."

"What?"

"Marry me. We can live together in college, you and me and Nell. I love you, Karma."

"No, Danny. I thought that was what I wanted, but I can't do this anymore. We aren't happy. We haven't been happy for a long time." Lakefield was speeding by. Had Aaryn watched us drive away? The clarity of what had to happen next felt amazing, like my life could be bright and clean again after all those weeks of fog.

"I love you so much," he said. "I'm going to do everything I can to make you happy."

"It's too late for that."

"What?" His voice actually shook.

"Please turn around and take me back to Aaryn's. It's over between us." My posture was straight. The words were sweet and empowering, a year in the making; a long, damaging year. He had fooled me and pushed me and almost ruined me, but I was strong. I was brave.

"I don't love you anymore."

CHAPTER 33

AARYN

Endlessness.

The clouds of Mount Olympus shifted above me. I was home. The city with honey-scented air, and light, and no Karma. The inhalation and exhalation of my breath was her name, as if I could hold on to her, hold on to life.

"Aaryn. Get up."

The marble was cold beneath my hands and feet as I tried to stand. I felt weak.

"Hey, Dad." But I couldn't. The ache of my human body had gone, but the ache for her was far worse. "I've lost her. I don't even know what to say."

"Who have you lost?"

I squinted, my head in my hand, but the brightness around me only changed shape.

My father clapped my shoulder. "Come on now, get up. You did it, son. You're finally home. I'm so proud of you."

"We need to talk about the arrows."

That's when I heard the murmur of the gods in the distance. A soothing hum of voices, like a calm, crowded arena, rose from a shadowed half-moon before us. There, tucked among storm clouds, the assembly had gathered.

"You did it," Dad repeated, grabbing my arm and leading me to where the white began to dissolve to gray. His golden cape flickered in the fog. Talk of my return grew louder, though I couldn't make out the words.

"No," I said. "I've failed you, and so many others, in so many ways. But we can fix things. Maybe the assembly can help us figure out what we're doing for people. What we stand for."

From the perimeter of light, Tek stepped forward. "I saw the chip register," he said.

I shrank back as if I could protect her memory from him by doing so.

"What chip?" Dad said. He'd crossed his arms at Tek's arrival, a little glance toward the heavens, where Zeus watched their interaction. As much as Dad hated Tek, everyone knew Zeus had a soft spot for the kid.

Tek stacked his arm across my shoulders, the material stinging. "The chip that's brought Aaryn home." He squeezed like we were buddies. "He'll be the next cupid joining High Tower."

"I won't." I shrugged out of his arm. "I'm done with this. I don't want to control people's lives, not with your software, or the arrows." I faced my father. "You don't know what you're doing to people. I saw what the arrows can do. What interfering can do. People deserve a choice in who they love."

She had been my choice. She would always be that. I felt short of breath as her name and face and smile filled my thoughts.

Tek and my father seemed more concerned with each other than with anything I had to say. They argued about whose side I was on. About the purpose of the cupids.

Dad's wings expanded with a rush, thick from his shoulder blades, rising into a curve along his face and sloping downward to points at the end. Smooth white feathers covered the wings' muscles in a clean pattern. "Love is a sacred thing," he told me. "Maybe someday you'll realize that."

"But the arrows are causing pain," I said. "They aren't only about love, are they, Dad?"

"What do you mean?"

"The practice arrow in my pack on finals. The lead arrow."

"What lead arrow?"

"I know about Mom."

My father stiffened. "Keep your mother out of this." In my peripheral vision, I saw a smirk rising on Tek's face.

I shook my head. "I know about Aleth. The lead arrow. Maybe a compatibility scan *would* be good for the arrows. Tek said he was working with you, which might actually be a good idea. We have to come up with a plan to help people instead of hurt them." A cruel thought came: that maybe they should all fall for someone who could never love them back. Maybe they'd get it. Let them try to live with the memory of someone they'd once loved.

"I like the sound of this," said a voice from the heavens.

Tek stepped forward. "But, Zeus, with all due respect—you and I both know there can only be one god of desire. Eros's own son believes the arrows are flawed. They're out of control. Dead arrows, lead arrows."

Tek needed to pay for his lies. "The Hive distracted me at the ration house on finals," I said. "Your program. So who's the one really out of control?"

"And the audit," Dad said, facing the heavens. "It seems like he's been working on this plan for a long time."

Tek's arms were crossed, his feet shifting.

"But have the arrows become strong enough to hurt people?" Zeus asked. "Eros, is it true that you used a lead arrow on your wife?"

"There was no lead arrow."

The sound of the wind filled my ears, roaring, the storm clouds building, mist hitting my face. "But Mom broke the arrow's spell," I said slowly.

"Yes." My father's wings drooped with a sigh, and he glanced at Tek, then me. "And I made up a myth about why we separated, to hide the truth. That Psyche fell in love with Aleth and broke her own spell."

CHAPTER 34

KARMA

I shivered as I stood outside Aaryn's apartment, knocking loudly.

He still hadn't answered, not the door, not my calls. I held my cheek to the wood and checked the handle, definitely locked. *Where are you, where are you, where are you, where—*

I sat on the doormat. The wind shook the entrance at the bottom of the stairwell, little ticking sounds from snow, cold seeping through the building. The way I'd left with Danny after that kiss, after everything. It was draining and exciting and I was really starting to worry that Aaryn might hate me.

I'm not sure how long my eyes were closed.

They opened at the sound of someone stumbling inside.

"Karma! You're here. But wait a minute, why? You left, and I—"

Aaryn stood at the bottom wearing khaki shorts, his chest naked. He held the railing as if moving might wake us from the moment.

His voice caught. "I thought you were gone."

The plastic fibers beneath my hand went flat, but I didn't rise, didn't know where to start.

"I broke up with Danny." I stared at him. "Why are you dressed like that? It's snowing." The light above the entry made his features sharp and beautiful.

He took one step forward, the snow in his hair already beginning to melt. "Because I'm human again, and for some reason they didn't send me with a shirt."

"Human again?"

The space between us began to feel like something I could choreograph, a real running at each other and spinning kind of moment. "I'm human now, but I used to be a god."

I laughed. "Well, that explains why you're so sculpted." And then my face got warm and I had to look away, though I kind of wanted to stare at his chest forever.

"I'm being serious. Before I came to Earth, I was a cupid on Mount Olympus."

I tilted my head to the side, one eyebrow raised.

"I'm the reason you stayed with Danny. My arrow, the one I shot you with a year ago, had you under a spell."

"*What?*"

"It's time."

"I'm pretty sure I'm the one in control of myself, thank you."

"You must have broken your own spell, like my mother did. I always knew you were strong."

"You're crazy."

"Crazy about you." The third stair creaked as he moved up, drops of water beading on his shoulders and chest. "I'm here now. Here to stay. The assembly let me stay." Fourth step. "I'm here to build a life—and I'm yours, if you'll have me." He nodded, like he was finally understanding something. "I belong here."

"The assembly? What are you talking about?"

"The assembly decides everything on Mount Olympus."

"You're insane!"

"Insane about you."

The wind quieted. Fifth step. "Longing for you." And my heart leapt hard because it had waited so long to give in to how I felt about him. My body felt like it was humming from the rush, the rush of letting myself care.

He held his elbows. "Freezing for you." And I chuckled, him drawing closer, closer, until only three steps and the landing separated us. He held out his hand. "Here for you."

"I never got to make my announcement." I smiled, feeling dizzy with excitement. "I got the scholarship."

He ran the remaining way and pulled me up for a kiss, which took my breath away; stupid as it sounds, that really happened. He hugged me too tight and spun around until I squealed, kissing my hair, my neck, both of my hands, really a crazy, insane guy.

"I can't believe it. Yes. Yes! I didn't totally screw up your life." And he kissed me again, his hands cupping my face, me half laughing as I kissed him back all sloppy, feeling happier than, I don't even know, just happy. "We have to celebrate, right now. We have to talk about everything, and I have to get a shirt on, and—there's so much to tell you. You have to promise you'll believe all the crazy parts, and then forgive me, no matter what."

"Oh my God."

"Yes?" He crowded me against the door gently, my arms winding around him, my lips inches from his. "I'm here."

ACKNOWLEDGMENTS

There's a saying for writers: "To you, your book is the world, but to the world, it is a book." I want everyone listed here to know that to me, *you are the world*. You and this book are connected. Thank you.

Thanks to my parents, Rick and Dawn, for giving me a happy childhood with plenty of time to imagine and write. To my grandparents, Jean, Larry, Virginia, David, and great–grandma Leona who were there, too.

To my sisters and best friends, Crystal, Tasha, Emily, and Laura, and my brother, Josh, for knowing me since they were born and loving me anyway. (BTW, I'm the boss.) To their spouses, Stef, Dusty, and JB.

To my husband, Shea, who deserves to be listed from beginning to end for everything he's done, from believing in me to cooking for me to reading early drafts. You love me so well.

To my parents-in-law, Doug and Kathy, for your endless support of me and my family. To Shel and Shem, too.

To Owen, Athena, and Avery. I love you. Whatever you become in the future, make it something good.

To my nieces and nephews, Cali, Lucy, Ari, Bryce, Gavin,

Hayden, Gabe, Brock, Laith, Ryder, Ledger, and Barrick, who fill my life with endless joy. Someday you'll be old enough to read this. Auntie will kiss your adorable cheeks until then.

To my friends and beta readers: Tracy Anderson, Susan Gray Foster, Alexa Donne, Carmen Baumann, and Miranda Paul. Your comments have made this book sing. Your friendship is invaluable.

To Sharon Verbeten and Molly Senechal, two of my favorite librarians, who read some of my earlier work. Your support has meant so much.

To Nate Perrigoue, who brought up the idea of cupids in the first place.

To those who helped further my careers at TP Printing and Gannett. I appreciate the opportunities I was given.

To Angie Flanagan, who helped me get the dance parts right.

To the SCBWI, especially the Wisconsin chapter, for all the help and encouragement along the way. Special thanks to the family of Marsha Dunlap, whose memorial scholarship allowed me to attend my first Fall Retreat. I hope there is some satisfaction in knowing you helped me follow my dreams.

To Carrie Howland, my literary agent, who has been my perfect match since we met on Twitter. XOXO forever.

To Wendy Loggia, my editor, who believed in *Arrows* when it was a much different book. She has transformed this story into something I find very beautiful and honest. Just think: in a way, you've given me the world. How cool is that?

To everyone at Penguin Random House who has helped bring this story into the world, especially Stephanie Moss, Colleen Fellingham, Tamar Schwartz, and Mary McCue.

To Ray Shappell for this genius cover.

To anyone who's ever felt lost loving someone who isn't right for them. Here is a good place to take a stand. Because, no—physical, emotional, and verbal abuse are not okay. Being with someone who holds you back in life is not okay.

Luckily, you are stronger than you think. You are brave.

Your choices can change everything.